THE PLACE OF SHELLS

Mai Ishizawa

The Place of Shells

translated from the Japanese
by Polly Barton

A NEW DIRECTIONS
PAPERBOOK ORIGINAL

The Place of Shells was originally published in 2021
as *Kai ni tsuzuku basho nite* by Kodansha Ltd., Tokyo.
Publication rights for this English edition arranged
through Kodansha Ltd., Tokyo.

First published as New Directions Paperbook 1621 in 2025
Manufactured in the United States of America

Library of Congress Cataloging-in-Publication Data
Names: Ishizawa, Mai, 1980– author. |
Barton, Polly (Translator), translator.
Title: The place of shells / Mai Ishizawa ; translated by Polly Barton.
Other titles: Kai ni tsuzuku basho ni te. English
Description: First edition. | New York, NY : New Directions Publishing
Corporation, 2025. | "A New Directions Paperbook."
Identifiers: LCCN 2024043471 | ISBN 9780811237789 (paperback) |
ISBN 9780811237796 (ebook)
Subjects: LCGFT: Novels.
Classification: LCC PL879.4.S55 K3513 2025 |
DDC 895.63/6–dc23/eng/20241030
LC record available at https://lccn.loc.gov/2024043471

2 4 6 8 10 9 7 5 3 1

New Directions Books are published for James Laughlin
by New Directions Publishing Corporation
80 Eighth Avenue, New York 10011

THE PLACE OF SHELLS

STANDING IN THE SHADE OF THE DESERTED STA-
tion, I awaited the arrival of a visitor whose face had half
vanished. Whenever I managed to sift through my memories
and cobble together some form of resemblance, it would slip
apart like water the next moment. Still I would continue,
gathering up the little pieces, forcing them inside the outline
of a head to create a collaged image. The repetition of this act
filled me with a sensation of cowardice, not unlike probing
an aching tooth with one's tongue over and over.

The early July sun grew ever whiter, unsparing in the heat
it exuded. Its rays oversaturated the colors of things, while
simultaneously returning everything to monochrome. In the
glistening white square in front of the station, there wasn't
a single shadow. People sat at a distance from each other on
benches, like stone statues able to withstand this heat without
melting. These figures, held transfixed by the sun, found their
contrast in the figure of a black dog weaving around them.
The dog was circling the transparent water that rose in jets
from the square. There were several fountains installed among
the cobblestones, from which water would spurt at irregular
intervals. Like plants made of glass with an impossibly fast life
cycle, the slender columns would shoot up to about the height
of a child, bloom and burst into flower and then quietly wilt
away, leaving only a dark circular stain behind. The dog twisted
its body joyfully as it cavorted with these watery snakes, glistening white and transparent. Each time the jets of water lost
their shape and shrank away, the dog would go bounding over
to a different fountain. Of every living thing in sight, he was

the only one who seemed to be enjoying himself, oblivious to the weight of the sun.

Beside the square of bleached cobblestones in front of Göttingen station lay a forest of interlocking bicycles. The bicycles had been intricately threaded into the gaps of the parking rack, the metal of their frames winking with a powerful light that even this sun was incapable of melting. Three years after first encountering it, I still didn't know how this complex physical structure maintained its balance. As I was watching, a cyclist approached and braked hard, slid the bicycle he'd been riding in one of the openings in the metal forest, and then came dashing toward the station. Deftly cloaking his face with his mask as he ran, he vanished inside the doors and was swallowed up by the building. That forest, now one vehicle more complex, had become such a dense mass that its appearance no longer seemed connected in any way to bicycles. As the light traced its surface, an image rose up in my mind of another kind of mound, assembled from those objects whose meanings have dissolved, and this too began to throb just like the toothache.

I checked the time and then peered inside the station through the front entrance. A train must have just arrived, as the once-empty station hall was now full of people, a rich burst of color filling its white space. As the travelers filed out the doors and moved off under the white rays of the sun, they too lost their pigmentation. I called the dog's name, and though he looked a little wistful to be dragged away from his game with the water, he came bounding straight over to where I stood. I fastened the leash to his collar and stepped inside the station. Inside the white entrance hall the dog's wet, black fur assumed a greater heft, its hue like a stake hammered into the whiteness, a post for me to lean on as I waited.

The people and their voices receded, even the voice over

the loudspeaker announcing the arrival of the trains was quiet, and for a brief moment the station hall stood in complete blankness. Stepping into the white from which all the sounds had vanished, I progressed a little farther down the corridor. The front and back entrances to the station were joined by a straight corridor, and if you looked around the several glass-fronted elevators positioned there, you could see all the way to the back entrance doors, small in the distance. Standing to one side of the hushed passageway, I trained my gaze in this direction, the bright green beyond, framed by the door, appeared to me as a painting. Its brightness did nothing to shrink the intervening distance between us, and as though I were staring down a telescope through the wrong end, the painting flickered in my vision like a fragment of a far-off world. As I focused upon it, a human figure slowly formed in my vision. There, in the corridor that distorted one's sense of perspective, stood Nomiya, his back to the green painting. He must've noticed me, and the monotonous squeak of his suitcase wheels drew closer. As the distance between us gradually lessened, I could tell that both the far-off time and my frozen memory had begun to thaw, creaking like those wheels. Nomiya's tall, slender figure seemed to shrewdly cast aside the heavy heat. His broad forehead and the positioning of his large eyes beneath it reminded me of a medieval statue. With the greenery flickering in the sun behind him, I thought for a moment of the stained glass renditions of saints that one saw in tall church windows.

Yet my memory was not moving smoothly. Nomiya now stood at speaking distance from me but with his mouth covered by a white mask, my impression of his face from the nose down was obscured by the color of that cloth. Beneath the span of white rendering his facial contours ambiguous, I couldn't perceive the movements of his mouth or the shapes of his words. My own face was similarly masked, and right now I felt very grateful for the fabric covering, even as it hotly obstructed my breathing. I too stayed buried behind the article concealing my mouth, resisting speech. I knew, however, that when we moved past the main entrance of the station, I would need to take it off, and then I would have to produce some words to connect his time and mine. Nomiya moved forward, casting off the impression of a saint imprisoned in glass, and finally, outside the station, he removed his mask. His mouth almost started to form some words that I thought must be, *It's been a long time*, yet perhaps his thoughts brushed up against the duration of time since the severance point, because in the end no sound came out, his mouth instead breaking into a slight smile. Seeing him bow his head to me in an understated yet polite gesture, a halting sense of pain welled up in me. My memories scattered in all directions and I lost my grasp on the words I'd been preparing. *Yes, this was how he greeted people* — the memories, which had been pieced together and then fell apart, now spoke. It was through his gestures, rather than his face or his body, that the nine-year gap was attempting to be bridged. At the same time, I felt a sense of relief to see the solidity of the form he took — solid enough, in fact, that the sun didn't shine through him. He may have been dead, but he still cast a shadow at his feet. Instead of speaking, I bowed my head back at him, as he had done. We both smiled sheepishly at the awkward reflexivity of my response, and now that our lips had moved, the conversation could naturally begin. *A long trip you've had*, I said, and Nomiya, understanding the multiple meanings that my sentence could carry, nodded and said, *Yes, I'm a little tired*, smiling unaffectedly. He went on to relate, in a calm tone of voice, how his train had been delayed and he'd missed his connection, and when looking for the next train to board he'd asked someone at the station for help, but they'd spoken too quickly, and their mask had muffled their voice, so he'd struggled to understand; and also to tell me of the castle he'd seen from the train window. From what he said, the way he talked about his trip, he sounded exactly like any normal traveler. Confronted by this firm sense of reality, the various things that I'd been imagining from speaking to Sawata, Nomiya's friend, dissolved into whiteness, and I found myself capable only of giving robotic responses. Eventually silence fell noisily upon this uneven exchange of ours, as if the cord holding up a heavy curtain had snapped.

There's lots of greenery, but I don't hear any cicadas, Nomiya mumbled, apparently unfazed by the way our conversation had broken off, narrowing his eyes as he peered into the sun in search of those voices that burnished the summer air. The heavy white light moved across his body, frozen in time, and yet his line of sight seemed somehow disconnected from the world in front of him: looking for the chirping of the cicadas that would fill the dense blankness, he directed his gaze on some far-off time.

The dog was observing Nomiya from a slight distance. His body language was easy enough to read: his tail, white only at the very tip, hung at an interim distance, showing his reservations. Not venturing beyond his own orbit, he waited for the other party to approach. I guessed he hadn't realized that Nomiya was a ghost, and yet it seemed his behavior toward any type of stranger was consistent, with no distinction between the living and the dead. Relieved to see this, I set off with Nomiya, down the road that led to the old town. Viewed from afar, we—the dog, Nomiya, and I—must have appeared to lose our color, to melt and vanish into whiteness. The whiteness blurred the perspective of memory, yet it couldn't completely fuse the rifts in time and distance.

Göttingen was a city that blended over the seams in time.

Immersed in overlapping memories, one could slip smoothly from one era to another. As in many German cities, the old town with its rich history lay at its center, and from there newer developments of the city spread out in all directions. The old town, approximately circular in shape, had once been encircled by defensive walls. Now in place of the walls, which had been knocked down, was a thin band of wooded area with a path weaving through it, well trodden by the feet of seasoned ramblers. It took about half an hour to walk from one end of the old town to the other, making it a good size to explore on foot, and walking through the streets lacing through the center, one was struck by the multifaceted structure of time there.

I'd found out through Sawata where Nomiya would be staying while he was here: north of the old town, near the University's Natural Sciences Department campus. "We should take the bus," I said, at which Nomiya nodded, and we moved down the wide street running along the wall that led away from the woods. There were buses that stopped outside the station, but none of them went directly to where Nomiya needed to go, so I'd decided to take him to the bus stop in the town center.

It was around two weeks ago that I'd heard that Nomiya would be coming to stay in Göttingen. To this day we hadn't exchanged any direct messages, relying instead on Sawata's polite, scrupulous intermediation. For that reason, I couldn't shake the feeling that I was here as Sawata's representative in this part of the world.

No sooner had we set foot in the old town, dragging our shadows behind us, than we came upon a golden orb gleaming dully in the sunlight. Positioned on the sidewalk next to a hotel with a pale stone facade, the orb looked like a bulging flower bud, swollen on its dark bronze stem. I saw Nomiya's eyes slowly taking it all in. *That's the Sun.* My voice, as it pronounced these words, seemed surprisingly far away, and I felt myself at risk of becoming disoriented.

Running through Göttingen was a Planetenweg—a planetary path—made up of scale models of the solar system. For a country so richly steeped in memories, these planetary models had only a short history, but they'd quickly become a fixture here, one of several symbols of the city. The path started out with the model of the Sun on Goethe-Allee, which ran in a straight line eastward from the station, and all the planets from Mercury to Neptune followed in order. The models' spacing from one another was dictated by the 1:2,000,000,000 scale at which they were rendered, and they therefore lay at assorted distances from one another—someone who wasn't paying attention could easily walk straight past without noticing them. Mercury through to Saturn lay within the bounds of the old town, while Uranus and Neptune were positioned surreptitiously in the residential area beyond. Neptune, at the end of the solar system, sat just at the border with the wood. The distances making up the solar system mapped fittingly onto the city's layout.

There were allegedly around fifty Planetenwegen in Germany alone, and sometimes it struck me as bizarre that people would want to create these small-scale versions of the solar system on Earth: Were we drifting further from space exploration, which had once formed the core of our sci-fi–tinged visions of the future? Or was it rather that now, Earth was so demanding of our attention that we had no choice but to keep our feet on the ground, and had to make do with these models as substitutes? In any case, whatever the reasoning behind the planets' installation, they made convenient landmarks for walkers and joggers, serving as signposts and markers of distance. Making their way along the line of planets, people moved toward or away from the Sun.

The bronze posts for the nine planetary bodies could appear at first glance like information panels for tourists, and as well as showing a simplified map of the Planetenweg that weaved through town, the panels displayed general information about the planets: their size, the duration of their orbit, their number of satellites, their distance from the Sun, and so forth. They also featured a scale model of the planet in question. The Sun, at the start, was represented as a large metal orb of burnished gold, its unstable form supported by the bronze rod beneath. It looked as though, if you kept staring at it, it might float up into the sky, like a balloon swollen in the sunshine. The models of the planets left a far less striking impression by comparison. At the top of each of the bronze posts was a peephole, in which the scale-model planets were displayed. From Mercury through to Mars, though, there was only a pinprick's worth of metal suspended in the thick glass. So small were these metallic heavenly bodies that, when one peered into the peephole's glass tarnished with fine scratches, one found they had been almost swallowed up and lost inside their distorted background. It was only beyond Mars that the planets began to command some kind of visual presence as objects.

Between the Sun and Mars, the distances between the planets were short. Nomiya and I walked along with the dog from the Sun to Mars, which took us about halfway down Goethe-Allee. Each time we came to one of the bronze posts Nomiya would pause to look, so the rhythm of our walking and the conversation that accompanied it assumed a discontinuous quality. We hadn't said much to one another since leaving the station. I knew that this was because of the nine-year distance between us, but I couldn't help feeling that the Planeten-weg, also, was responsible for impeding our conversation. Yet, somewhere, I welcomed this situation. These bronze markers helped to paper over the gaps in our communication, which lay closer to silence than dialogue.

Over the river, the name of the road changed to Prinzenstrasse, yet the transition from Goethe to Prince heralded no discernible difference to the appearance of the street: for a while there were no bronze posts and, feeling suddenly flustered by the empty spaces in our conversation, I began delivering an incoherent monologue about the town. To the left, I pointed as we walked along, there was a secondhand bookstore, a place serving stone-baked pizzas, a musical instrument shop and a stationery shop, and on the right, the library, standing solitary and silent. Finally, next to the florist and the old bookstore facing onto the central street that ran from north to south through the old town, we encountered the bronze post for Jupiter.

It was Agatha's dog that I'd brought out with me to meet Nomiya. Agatha was my roommate—for a year and a half now, we'd been renting a place together. She'd studied economics at Hamburg University, worked briefly at an office job, then moved to Göttingen to study information science.

Her dog was the size of a beagle, his longish fur divided into clearly defined black-and-white sections, with no blurring of the two. Most of his face and back was black, while his belly, legs, chest, and neck, as well one section of his tail, were white. His snout was longish, and his face had an indistinct look, as if that of another animal had been grafted onto it.

Most people—except Agatha—referred to him as the "truffle dog." Our ears and our tongues were more accustomed to that nomenclature than to his real name, which was Hector. Just as one might suspect, a truffle dog is a dog with a talent for sniffing out truffles. Having undergone training to sniff out that particular scent from beneath the ground, truffle dogs possess the ability to dig up those fungi. Agatha's dog had been trained to recognize the smell by his former owner, Agatha's mother, who'd lived with the dog in a small village far south of Göttingen, where she'd enjoyed the leisurely forest walks and hikes, which were her main pastime. She'd died a year and a half earlier of breast cancer.

It was not only the truffle dog that Agatha had inherited from her mother, but also the mythology surrounding the creature. The small village where Agatha's mother lived was half submerged in forest, which was home to those pungent fungi, secreted underground. In late summer, three years ago, on his daily walk in the forest, Hector had found a black truffle. He'd wrinkled up his long snout, dived without warning into the thicket and begun pawing at the ground with his nose glued to the ground. As Agatha's mother watched, he proceeded to unearth a round, black object from the soil. That fertile-smelling black object was small enough, yet heavy and dense. Agatha's mother had put it in her pocket to take home. Harvesting naturally growing truffles was forbidden in Germany, for environmental protection. *One could be overlooked, though, surely*—so Agatha's mother had said with a smile. Yet as it turned out, the excavation wouldn't be a onetime occurrence.

After noticing the dog nuzzling at her pocket, where the scent of the truffle still lingered, Agatha's mother repeatedly brought the truffle up to his nose, thus imprinting the smell memory in the dog. The forest was a symphony of scent: the verdure, and the water it contained; the fallen leaves that had turned to mulch, and the mold rotting the backs of the leaves; the soil dissolving in the warmth of the sun; the smell of the cool green tinged with the young freshness of cedar; the dry aroma of the deciduous trees with their deeply stacked layers of fall colors. Now, the hue of this truffle scent had been added to the composition. In the dog's olfactory purview, the forest appeared with clarity. Yet, just as it is impossible to isolate each color of an impressionist painting, so the nature of that composition remained a secret known to just the dog and the forest. The dog, who came from that point on to be known as the truffle dog, never excavated more than three truffles at a time. He's respectful of the forest, Agatha's mother would say, burying her fingers in the dog's wispy, soft black fur and smiling.

After Agatha's mother's death, Agatha brought the truffle dog to Göttingen where she was living, and the dog slowly began to adapt to this new environment. Göttingen, too, was enveloped by forest. The remains of the medieval wall encircling the city made for a good walking route, and Agatha would take the truffle dog with her around the loop of forest. Every time I saw a dog owner with their dog bounding around at their feet, I'd think of a planet moving along its orbit, with its satellite in tow. On weekends she'd sometimes venture further afield, and had gotten into the habit of going to the woods beyond the green space where the Neptune post stood. Agatha didn't appear to have many expectations when it came to finding truffles, but we'd often joke with each other that if he did find one, we'd keep it as our secret. She'd shown me a photograph of a truffle the dog had found the year before her mother's death. A small thing encased in a black, scaly skin, strongly resembling a burned-out star that had come tumbling down from the sky.

We'd spoken so much about the truffle dog that our conversation had come to assume the taste and flavor of the spherical black fungus. Through these anecdotes, my nose and my mouth were attempting to summon up their own impressions of this unfamiliar, meteorite-like object. The word, *truffle*, was starting to move on its own, taking steps all by itself, like some ghost possessing my senses of smell and taste.

I continued reeling off little stories and anecdotes, moving from the city to the truffle dog without settling into a single train of thought, as if playing a game of word association. Taking advantage of Nomiya's quiet receptivity, words that emulated Agatha's stories came tumbling from my mouth. The narratives that come tumbling forth were fabrications—deceptions, in a sense. This was a bad habit of mine, digressing about animals as a kind of conversation filler to evade the central issues. The very reason I'd brought the truffle dog along with me was to serve as a kind of first aid kit, in case our conversation fell apart at the seams. When my words finally ran out, both Nomiya and I stayed silent, pretending to be captivated by what the truffle dog was doing. He was more or less keeping pace with us and didn't otherwise provide any hints for what to say next. I kept that nine-year expanse of time in the periphery of my vision as I circled around its edge, taking care not to encroach upon it directly. Maybe Nomiya was doing the same. However I strained my ears, I couldn't fathom the depth of his silence.

Reaching the Jupiter post, we turned left and passed north through the town center. Weender Strasse dissected the old town into west and east sides. The street was pedestrian only except for postal vans, garbage trucks, and police vehicles, so it was largely only the footsteps of walkers that encroached on its cobbles.

With Jupiter behind us, we strayed away from the Planetenweg. When he'd seen the scale model of Jupiter suspended in the bronze post—the first of the planets with any sense of material presence—Nomiya had traced its outline lightly with a finger. My memory let out a creak, as it came back to me that this was something he'd always done when describing a work of art: as his words narrated the contents of a picture or a sculpture, his fingertips would move across the surface of the table or through the air, describing outlines and positions, as though he were attempting to engrave the memory into his fingers as well.

"We should head to the bus stop, so unfortunately our tour of the planets will have to stop with Jupiter."

"Are we far from Saturn?"

"Yes, it's a way off in that direction. It's positioned at the edge of the old town. You should go and see it some time." Nomiya lifted his finger unsentimentally from Jupiter and walked on, proceeding without hesitation through the clamor of the city that reverberated with words of an unfamiliar cadence.

The crowds were returning to Weender Strasse, but people now walked in a way that demonstrated an awareness of their distance from others, and there were more solo pedestrians than before. "There's not so many people, for a main street like this," Nomiya said quietly, running his eyes down the road. I'd explained the situation here when I spoke with Sawata, but I didn't know how much of that had been passed on to Nomiya. Since March, the shadow cast by that unfamiliar word — Covid" — had been morphing into terrifying shapes the moment you took your eyes off it. "There was a mass outbreak last month, so we've backtracked again. There'll be more people around again soon," I replied, and he nodded. That surge in cases, just as the restrictions had been easing, had made an immediate impact on the atmosphere in the city. Now things were relaxing once again, but I couldn't shake the memory of the bewilderment of that period, like an opened door being slammed shut in one's face. The abrupt shift from deregulation to increased vigilance drove a large crack through one's sense of reality, and a sensation not dissimilar to jet lag rendered everything hazy. In theory, of course, I understood full well how precarious reality was, and yet it seemed I still maintained an unconditional belief in the stability of its foundations. Perhaps Sawata had already provided him with some information, because Nomiya asked no further questions, taking in the city as his feet crossed from sunlight into shade. I didn't offer up any more explanations about the irreal situation that had endured here for some months, but simply gave a him a list of the rules and regulations as they currently stood. Maybe it wasn't words that he needed to bridge the gap between him and reality—maybe the adjustment had to be a sensorial one. Just how did one go about accustoming to a time difference of nine years? How did this place—this distorted, tranquil, otherworldly way of life—appear through Nomiya's eyes?

As we were walking, the truffle dog began nudging my leg with his nose, registering his thirst. I took out a bowl and a bottle from my backpack, and poured out some now-warmish water for the desperate, thirsty animal. At the sound of the pouring water, louder than I'd expected, I felt my body contract, and snuck a glance in Nomiya's direction. He was gazing up at the buildings lining the street, his attention apparently diverted. The facades of the buildings were studded with faces, which looked down at Nomiya, returning his gaze. The faces—a man with a funny smirk, an indignant devil—functioned much like masks, staring fixedly out on the town. I hadn't yet developed any distinct thoughts about these faces that studded the exteriors of buildings and haunted the facades of houses. I supposed that in time, they would become as much a part of my own temporal reality as the faces of family members—or else, I would come to perceive them as something belonging to the other side, treating them like unfortunate lodgers, resident ghosts.

Near the border of the old town was a large mall containing clothes shops, a drugstore, a supermarket, etc. There was an electronics and appliances shop named Saturn in there too—so we had, in some sense, reached the sixth planet, albeit in an alternate form. I asked Nomiya if he needed to do any shopping, but he replied that he'd already researched and memorized the necessary information about grocery stores and pharmacies near his accommodation in the north of the city. Across the street was a line of several bus stops; as people had started to leave their homes again, the buses had once more resumed their normal schedules. Judging by Nomiya's unhesitating movements, it seemed that he had grasped the location of the bus stop as well. I stood there awkwardly with the truffle dog, like a child in an elementary school play given the kind of background role identified by a number or a letter. Unable to serve even as guide to the city, all I'd really done was meet Nomiya and walk with him along the Planetenweg as far as Jupiter.

A bus heading in the direction of Nomiya's accommodation in the north approached almost immediately. I felt a sense of relief when he managed to board the bus safely, amid the flow of stock phrases and gestures I'd opted to use instead of all the other words I couldn't seem to string together. I watched him through the window as he drifted away—his seated figure, his eyes. Once the bus had gone, I felt myself short of breath, and inhaled several times deeply. Since meeting him at the station, I had been breathing exclusively through my mouth, forcing a very unnatural rhythm upon my body. This was all part of an attempt to block out any smells or odors that he might have been emitting. All this time, I'd been scared that he might have been carrying the smell of the sea, or even the smells associated with death.

After parting with Nomiya, I turned and walked back in the direction I'd come, approaching the spot where Weender

Strasse met with the Planetenweg, the bronze post for Jupiter visible in the distance. The truffle dog trotted along obediently, inside my shadow.

The town's navel, situated where the Planetenweg running from west to east through the old town intersected with Weender Strasse running from north to south, was a bronze sculpture titled *Der Tanz* (*The Dance*). Three figures—a man, woman, and child—were positioned as if dancing in a circle, but there was no trace of elegance or exuberant musicality to their movements. Instead, portrayed here was unquestionably some kind of combat—or at least a marital fight or family conflict. The man and woman were grasping at each other's faces, while contorting their bodies to avoid the hands reaching for them. The bronze muscles cresting on their exposed arms and chests testified to the oppositional forces residing in the bodies that were vying to turn their faces from each other. In their hands, they held the masks that they'd torn from each other's faces. The child, clinging to the mother's side, stretched out a hand to tug at the hem of the man's clothing. The dance of the title, presumably, referenced the feeling of momentum generated by this silent, bronze-cast struggle. Before rejoining the Planetenweg and making my way toward Saturn, I looked once again at those dancing figures, positioned close to Jupiter.

Heavy beneath the stark rays of sun, the dancers were not spinning around, but taking aim at each other's faces. Was showing each other their true, unmasked faces really something that necessitated this much tension, this bitter a struggle? Amid all the attempts to feel out the insides, the words, even the aura of the other, reading the look on their face is surely the simplest option. Perhaps the idea that what lies beneath a mask is one's real face, where a person's true feelings are shown, is an article of collective, unyielding faith. Yet as more time passes, and multiple masks build up upon a face, the task of stripping them off only grows ever harder.

Nor was this true simply of human faces. Memories and places, too, assume masks. In memory, particularly, the mask of nostalgia is applied to people and places: that dreamy countenance created by distant times and places, sometimes accompanied by pain.

There are occasions, though, when not just the mask, but the face itself is peeled off. Sometimes the face and the memories of a certain time held by a place are cruelly ripped away, the traces of that destruction affixed there, instead of a face. In my memories, too, what lingers on and on is that ravaged visage.

Nomiya was one of those who had disappeared on that day in March, many years ago.

In Sendai, where I grew up, March hovered on the borderline between winter and spring. If the sun appeared to soften things, the air retained a silent frigidity at its core; if there was warmth in the air, it was belied by the gray of the sky, redolent with the heaviness of winter. The colors that your eyes perceived failed to align with what you felt on your skin. As you attempted to make sense of this rift between vision and sensation, spring would spread as if dissolving through the world, all the colors melting—until a big snowfall came to return everything to white again.

March 11, 2011, was one such day when we were abruptly pulled back to the gray of winter. From the middle of the afternoon, after the violent tremors and rumbling pushing up from deep in the earth, the Tohoku area and its vicinity was cut off from everything. It was then that the wall of water came pressing in from the sea, swallowing up the coastal area. The wall enveloped everything, surging inland with a momentum that eclipsed past experiences and records, engulfing people and houses and forcefully wresting them away from the land before receding back in the direction of the sea.

Being at home as I was that day, in my family's house up in the mountains, I experienced the tremors dragging on, the heavy bass rumbling the earth. The quaking made cracks appear in the walls of our house. Most of the tiles in the bathroom cracked and fell off, the books came flying from the shelves, various pieces of furniture toppled over, and almost all our tableware broke. Fearing the chaos indoors, I escaped outside with my sister, who'd been in bed with the beginnings of a cold, and our dog. The electricity and gas stopped before the end of the day, and the water the following day. No information reached us, either.

I'd never lived near the sea, so the possibility of a tsunami didn't even cross my mind. The anxiety about the tremors and the destruction had left the inside of my head completely blank. In addition to my distance from the sea, I suppose another reason that the danger of a tsunami didn't occur to me was my conviction that the earthquake was a recurrence of the earthquake whose epicenter lay in offshore Miyagi, as had been predicted. Tsunamis hadn't featured in my parents' accounts of their memories of the previous Miyagi quakes, after all. At that time, I was far more concerned about the destruction to the inland region. I had no concept of what might occur after the tremors subsided, and in my panic and confusion, I kept my eyes glued to my cell phone, which was refusing to connect me to my parents. By the time the aftershocks hit, information was already becoming scant. The temporal and geographical severance had already begun.

That night, I managed to move enough of the scattered

books out of the way to crawl into bed, still in my clothes, glaring continuously at the screen of my phone. The screen informed me that 300 bodies had washed up on Arahama Beach. Then it fell silent. This tiny window of information that had been struggling to remain open finally shut, leaving me in a place of obscurity and confusion. It was then that, for the first time, the faces of my friends living by the coast rose to my eyes, tainted by the anxiety and fear induced by the totality of the blackout. These images ruffled my consciousness, ravaged faces floating within the profound darkness spreading around me that remained the same whether I opened or closed my eyes. In the pauses between the voices on the radio that I could hear coming faintly from my parents' room, the quiet reverberations of my sister's coughing echoed out through the night. I still couldn't reach several of my friends. As I lay listening to the night's deep breathing, like the distant rumble of the earth, my body remained vigilant, poised for action. Downstairs, the dog would whimper in fright with each aftershock.

That night, I floated around in a shallow sleep, waking with each tremor, and in that absolute darkness, I would push the button of my phone whose only functions were now those of dim illumination and clock. In the bed I'd thrown myself in without changing into the nighttime skin of my pajamas, the thick denim of my jeans and the bulkiness of my sweater scuffled with the blankets, pushing sleep still further away. I tried burying my ears in the pillow, but I could still hear the faint rumbling, trapped inside my head like a ringing. Unable to sleep in such complete darkness I opened the curtains, but the streetlights stood there forlornly—there was no light to be seen from outside either. Yet in the midnight sky shone a sprinkling of ruthlessly beautiful stars, still and fierce. Up there, facing this one, was a world of peace and tranquility. My line of sight, which had wandered automatically upward to the sky, was struck by its glow and disappeared. I was still totally incapable of imagining what was going on below.

After some days had passed, I was able to access some fragmentary information.

Nomiya had been in his house in Ishinomaki on that day. The town's fishing port floated in miniature inside the window frame of his second-floor bedroom, the gently breathing sea melding into the scenery of daily life. He had lived alongside it—lived with images of both its quiet and its bleakness forever superimposed in the recesses of his vision. In the time that accumulated inside him, his ears would have stored up the sound of the distant sea like conch shells, and his tactile, olfactory, and other sense memories must also have been interwoven with it.

None of my friends had been able to piece together Nomiya's movements that day. When Sawata had gotten in touch with him on the 9th, Nomiya mentioned meeting up with an old friend who was back in town, paying a visit to family and friends. He'd exchanged a few brief words with Sawata about the earthquake that took place just after lunchtime. But we couldn't trace his steps after that, couldn't work out where and how he'd been swallowed up by the water. Our hopes of understanding how his final moments had been remained unfulfilled.

Nomiya's house had been entirely desecrated by the tsunami, and all of his family members had been swallowed up by the wall of water, separately from one another. His family didn't have any close relatives, and most of their local acquaintances had also lost their lives to the tsunami. The sea, which had remained a stable presence throughout the majority of Nomiya's time, hadn't left behind even the slightest trace of their memories. His younger sister's body was discovered at the beginning of April, and at the end of July, his father was pulled from the water. Three years later, his mother had finally been returned. Yet nine years afterward, Nomiya and his younger brother still hadn't been recovered from the sea.

Saturn lay some distance from Jupiter, which was located centrally in the old town. If you continued down the Planetenweg after Prinzenstrasse turned into Theaterstrasse, you would encounter its bronze post. It was close to the gap in the city wall walking loop, and to the Deutsches Theater. The theater was enveloped in green, and since spring this year, had sat there silently, hunkered down in the expressionlessness of its stone. The restaurant attached to the theater, too, had been wiped of its expression, with the glass windows across the entirety of its front facade reflecting the green of the forest.

Turning midway off the Planetenweg that led toward Saturn, the truffle dog and I took a shortcut back to my apartment. About twenty minutes' walk along the path tracing where the city wall had once stood was a four-story house of a warm yellow shade, and it was in an apartment on its second floor that the dog and I lived together. The circular band of forest encircling the city traversed its official border and encroached on the territory of our house, creeping into the windows. Through spring and summer, the haphazardly intertwined plants would occasionally burst into flower, but mostly it was just foliage.

As soon as I opened the front door, the truffle dog bounded into the living room, sensing Agatha's presence. Contorting his body in delight at his reunion with Agatha after a week apart, he whirled round and round. Agatha had been visiting her sister in Cologne, and had asked me to take care of the dog in her absence. Very little had been required of me, other than giving him food and water and taking him for walks.

While Agatha had been away, the truffle dog spent his time rotating between the coolest spots in the flat, before choosing one of them to fall asleep in. Perhaps the heat had made him indolent, or else he was just missing his owner—in either case, he seemed to have morphed into a black rug, which moved around the apartment and slept in different places. Even when I rested a hand on his belly, which rose and fell with the tide of his gentle breathing, he wouldn't wake. The only thing I received was a smooth sensation that reminded me of water. The dog quite clearly didn't want to interact with me.

Agatha had sat down on the sofa, the truffle dog still excitedly circling around her. Seeing me, she said hello and smiled, but her facial expression seemed somehow disjointed from this greeting. Some people, returning from being away, forget to bring their faces back with them immediately. Perhaps owing to an inability to fathom the passage of time in absentia, their faces only catch them up after some time has passed, like pictures drawn in invisible ink, or an item of luggage collected later. Yes, there was a lag in time about Agatha's expression—not only due to the exhaustion of the trip, I surmised, but because she was seeing reality through a peephole while her mind was focused intently on something else. Hers was the face of someone looking at two different times simultaneously, an expression similar to the one that nearly everyone I knew had worn since that day in March.

"How was it to get away, after so long?"

"Tiring, more than anything. I never realized that traveling consumed so much energy. At first everything I was seeing seemed so bright and vivid, but after a while I felt like I couldn't process it all. I developed a kind of mental indigestion."

"How was Cologne? Did it seem different?"

"Not especially. I expected things would be different in another place, but it's basically the same as here. Busy, as well. I guess I was hoping to sense some definitive distinction between there and here, but there wasn't really. The distance between people feels like it's shrinking, too."

The truffle dog was digging into the food that had already been put out for him, his back turned to us. As I listened to Agatha speaking about her sister, I felt a particular perception tugging at me. Every time the subject turned to her dead mother, Agatha would display an odd hesitancy, as if she had a toothache. Distracted by this thought, I found my mind drifting, until her voice asked me where I'd been with the truffle dog, which pulled me back to my consciousness. "We went to collect Nomiya's ghost from the station," I made to say, then stopped myself. That was a strange way of putting it, I thought. Saying "Nomiya's ghost" made it seem as though the ghost were different from Nomiya himself—as though it were just one dislocated part of him. Yet how else could I word it? "Dead Nomiya" only invited thoughts with an unpleasant aftertaste. Using a modifier like that felt like I was forcing his head down, trying to tidy him away and out of sight. "I went to see someone I attended university with," I said, playing it safe and not mentioning the intervening nine years. At that moment the truffle dog, who was licking his bowl, lifted his head and shot me a glance, a strangely thoughtful look in his eyes.

That night, around four hours before the date changed, I had a call from Sawata on Skype. Back at university in Sendai, both he and I had been Western art history majors. His research topic was seventeenth-century French art, with a focus on Nicolas Poussin, and after graduating with his MA he'd taken a job as a curator in an art museum in his home city of Yamagata.

Sawata and Nomiya studied together at university, and had been extremely close. Nine years ago, Sawata had gone back to

Sendai in mid-April, registering as a volunteer aid worker and heading for the coastal region. Our inability to get in touch with Nomiya, and the fact that the house where he'd been living near Ishinomaki had endured irreparable damage, had borne an icy conviction inside us, even if we didn't vocalize it. Sawata tried speaking to as many as people as possible, to all of the volunteers, police, and other emergency services personnel from the area where Nomiya's house had been, to see if they had any news about him. Yet the Senseki Line connecting Sendai with Ishinomaki had been destroyed by the tsunami, making visiting there very difficult. It took a fearsome amount of time to travel to the places that had been cut off from one another.

Sawata barely spoke to us about what he'd seen there, after all our connections with Nomiya had been severed. The scenes of destruction remained floating in his vision. I imagined that still today, those vestiges of lives that had been driven into great mounds of rubble—the vestiges that served to erase all names and all the meanings attaching to things, and the memories that these evoked—lingered there at the back of his sight. Sawata had visited the area where Nomiya's house had been, and sensed directly—been made to sense directly—the death of his friend, engulfed and rendered indistinguishable from others who had met the same fate. Their deaths went on to become a reality—a reality that was premised upon the fact that there'd been no place, no opportunity to view the dead as individual people, and in most cases, there wasn't even so much as a body. Having wandered around that place at that time, Sawata now carried those severed words and memories inside himself. Quite probably, they refused to embed themselves in the flow of passing time, and instead remained suspended inside him.

It was Sawata who'd told me that Nomiya would be coming

to Göttingen. Nomiya had gotten in touch with him, after a hiatus of nine years. In a situation like this, I didn't know how Nomiya would have proved that he was on the other end of the line, when the natural thing would've been to assume the call was a scam of some kind. I couldn't imagine what the conversation would have been like, or how disoriented and confused Sawata must have been. When Sawata called to let me know, his demeanor had been matter-of-fact, and we'd communicated afterward only a few brief times.

I knew that his call that evening was to confirm Nomiya's arrival. With the time difference, he must have been immersed in the dark heavy blue of predawn, but both he and I kept our cameras off. We both felt a vague antipathy toward seeing the expressions that came over our own and each other's faces when speaking about Nomiya. Yet the absence of visual information in our chat made the links between our words, the expressivity lurking in our tone, and our hesitations starker. Without the need to read the expression of the person on the other side of the screen, our ears naturally homed in on the unsaid, on trying to interpret the spaces between words.

Sawata listened to my report, a string of simple scenes describing the time from our first meeting at the train station to seeing him off at the bus stop. Then he paused. After digesting this he said, in a voice whose contours seemed hard to place: "... Did he seem the same?"

If Sawata had heard from Nomiya two weeks previously, he must have formed an impression of how he was doing, even if only vaguely. I imagined that what he wanted to know was whether, visually speaking, the nine-year rift in time had left an imprint on the Nomiya who'd stepped across it, had changed that Nomiya somehow, or if he remained unaltered from how he was nine years back. The idea that, in a way, both Sawata and I conceived of Nomiya not as a dead person but a castaway from the past spread through my mind like a bleeding stain.

I now thought back to earlier that afternoon when I'd met him at the station—to that saintlike figure who appeared against the entryway enclosed in green. As we'd followed the route of the Planetenweg, I'd found that, even when I went to turn my eyes upon the face of the person walking next to me, my focus would be fixed upon the city behind him. The Nomiya impressed upon my memory was blurry and hard to discern, like a photograph that wasn't in focus. I hadn't been able to catch a clear glimpse of him when he'd gotten on the bus either, obscured as he was by the other passengers' heads. Since my knowledge of Nomiya was only from the research faculty we shared, I didn't have any likeness of him embedded deep in my memory, with which I could compare him as he was currently. Though I was supposedly trying to convey my impressions of Nomiya, I found myself talking about him as if I were describing an icon. I heard Sawata's quiet, slightly sarcastic laugh from the other side of the dark, flat screen, on a slight delay.

"You sound like you're reading out the description of an artwork from a catalog."

"Sorry. I don't feel like I can look at him properly yet, across the distance of nine years."

"I know. Stacking up metaphors and images is the only way we have of describing him, because that's the least painful way of thinking about him. All that training we went through to enable us to hold several pictures in our mind's eye at the same time becomes an obstacle when trying to see a person as they actually are . . . I wonder, though, whether I truly want to know what he's like now. You know? I just don't know. If he's exactly the same as he was before, I guess I'll feel a temporal separation, since I've aged and changed over time. On the other hand, if he has changed, I'm slightly terrified by the prospect that those changes would overwrite the image that I have of him, in a way. He can't picture at all what these nine years have been like for us. That vision of the land heaped with rubble is imprinted so powerfully inside me—imagery that then transformed itself into words that rang out in my ears, telling me that he hadn't survived. The picture of him in my memory has been obscured by the sight of that place, so I can't properly recall his face. I guess I'm confused about whether this means he's returned or—or if it doesn't mean that at all. Sorry."

Sawata's voice became a sigh, then burrowed quietly into the silence. For a moment I thought that the connection was bad and I couldn't hear him, but then I realized he was awaiting a response from me, the words themselves having grown hesitant. Sawata had only communicated with Nomiya by messages and Skype, had only interacted with him by text and voice. When it came down to it, neither of us had seen Nomiya. Something hidden at the back of Sawata's voice told me that he was unable to adapt to the nine-year time gap.

"Oh, I wanted to ask you something else: Would Akiko come, do you think? If we told her."

Now Sawata unexpectedly changed the subject. Akiko had been part of the same research faculty as us, and now lived in Ghent. She was about the only one of our cohort who was in any way proximate to Göttingen, but neither Sawata nor I had told her anything yet.

"It might be difficult to travel here from Belgium. The national borders have only just opened up, and I doubt she'd be able to leave at a moment's notice. It's a very unsettled period."

It was at times like these that one became conscious of national borders, that those invisible seams between nations rose up into focus. In a place like Europe, which was hard to grasp in its entirety, people's sense of the distance between places was inevitably somewhat vague, but for those who were here on a visa, as I was, those distances remained perpetually far-off. Ironically, it was now more difficult to meet up with my friends who were living than with those who were dead.

After another silence, Sawata's voice, now seemingly bereft of contours, said, So I'm guessing Nomiya won't be back by mid-August? Perhaps interpreting my silence to be forgetfulness, Sawata squeezed out another word, somewhat bewildered: Obon. Obon, the festival when the spirits of the dead would return to the earth, began in a month and a half. As to whether Nomiya would remain here or "return home" for that festival, I didn't have the faintest idea.

"He doesn't have a place to return to. Or anyone to welcome him home," Sawata murmured, forlornly. His voice seemed mismatched with the smiling face in his profile photo, a circle floating against the black background of the screen. I'd heard that Nomiya didn't have any blood relations aside from his immediate family who'd all been swallowed up by the sea. Maybe the fact that he's appearing like this is a sign that his body will be found, Sawata suggested to me casually before that, too, dissolved inconclusively. I said nothing.

Now that both of us had lost the will to carry on the conversation, the silence took up more space than the words. When we ended the call, I felt a lightness that came from the relief of having concluded my report on the day, while also noticing the weight of Sawata's words that were only now properly sinking in. In the attempt to rip off the masks we were wearing, we'd gone round and round in circles. It was already past half ten. Meeting with Nomiya had stirred up memories that had been fading away and I felt stumped at being confronted by these feelings that had no outlet. Glancing at the calendar, I saw the day after tomorrow was Thursday. Thursday afternoon was the time that Ursula kept free. To her friends and acquaintances who visited, she offered tea and cake, and a comfortable silence in which to talk. Since June, restrictions on meeting with people and being in one another's houses had eased, which meant her time and her home had been opened up once again. The visitors, who referred to themselves as Thursdayers, now came not all at once, but at their allotted time slots. *Can I come to see you on Thursday?* Texting her, I requested a slice of Ursula's time.

It was through Ursula that I'd met Agatha. Within the small city of Göttingen, Ursula had built up an incredibly wide-reaching network of connections. When you began to plot the relationships she'd formed with people both inside and outside the city using points and lines, it came to resemble the diagram of a complex stellar constellation.

For decades, Ursula had taught German and literature at a prep school. She wasn't one of those teachers who became particularly close to her students, one of those who lit up the classroom with a sparkling sense of humor or engaged with the students in a placid, easygoing manner. She was distinguished but strict, and the tests she gave were difficult. It was her perpetual goal to rub out and amend mistakes, which she saw as stains on the memory. Yet she was loved by her students, and people naturally gravitated to her. After retiring and beginning to live off her pension, she chose a life buried in books, and joined a small reading group. There, too, rather than opining passionately, she would keep her mouth shut and listen, intervening gently to share some brief thoughts only when the conversational thread grew tangled. For this reason, although the reading group may not have greatly broadened her literary horizons, she gained many new acquaintances from it. The women in the book club were added to her existing social circle, which consisted of former students who'd assumed the position of friends, as well as her old acquaintances and neighbors. Sometimes people visited her just to have a chat, and at other times they wanted to talk to her about something specific. It seemed that the secret to her gravitational pull lay not in her words, but in her silence. Those who held unspoken words inside themselves flocked to her.

Over time Ursula's constellation of relationships grew ever more complex, because through her, the people visiting and seeking counsel from her inevitably formed more connections with one another. When someone was looking for a good ophthalmologist, or needed materials from a specialist library in another city's university, or was after a Spanish tutor, Ursula would introduce one of her acquaintances, as though pointing out a particular star. When I was looking for a proofreader for my thesis, she introduced me to Katharina, whose research was in philosophy, and when I was thinking of moving, she put me in touch with Agatha, who was looking for someone to rent an apartment with.

I was another one of those people who'd been incorporated into Ursula's star chart. This had happened because one day, I discovered on a bulletin board at the library that there was an upcoming reading group discussing Natsume Soseki's *Ten Nights of Dreams*. When I showed up at the address from the handwritten poster, I found only three people in the room. Two of the three were twittering away like birds, yet it wasn't at each other that their words were directed, but the third person sitting silently beside them. In spite of her thin, petite frame, she had a solid, reassuring presence, and her eyes would occasionally glint with potent pleasure, in a way that reminded me of dappled sunlight falling through the leaves. Overall, she had the silent calm of a tree. Even once the very earnest student who'd organized the group had arrived and opened up the book, the same avian twittering and arboreal silence continued as before. When occasionally a voice like the rustling of leaves emerged from the tree's mouth, the birds would pause their singing. This treelike person was Ursula. When the discussion had continued for some time, she turned to me and asked, "If you saw a flower blooming for the first time in a hundred years, would you believe that you were being reunited with someone who'd died?" In the end, we only discussed the first dream that day. Nor did we make great progress after that either—some attendees dropped out and new ones joined—and the *Ten Nights of Dreams* reading group only made it to the fourth night's dream before it eventually disbanded. And over this time, I switched from attending the reading group to visiting Ursula's house.

Ursula's building faced onto Judenstrasse, along which the buses passed noisily. Judenstrasse was a main road running through the town parallel with Weender Strasse, not far from the Jupiter post. On that street lay a plain, inconspicuous-looking gate. First, you passed through a courtyard, like a cross between a forest and a small garden. Cut off from the clamor of the street, it was so hushed here that you found your ears throbbing in the void. The apartment itself was one of the buildings that sheltered the courtyard from the outside.

When you went to see Ursula, there would always be a cheesecake waiting on a large plate on the table. Its firm crust baked to a golden brown was filled with soft, pale-yellow cream cheese. Dusted with cocoa and cinnamon powder, its surface formed an unusual marble pattern. As soon as you sat down, you'd be served a slice of cake. Most of the people who came to her were those whose threads, whose time, whose memories had grown tangled in some way. Unable to locate the end of the conversational thread, many suffered from a kind of lexical indigestion. Ursula's Käsekuchen served as a lubricant to help them move their mouths, their tongues. The women who flocked in large numbers to her apartment would eat the cake, allowing Ursula to spool their thread for them. Many of her visitors needed her silence, and there were always new faces being added to the array. Just like with the moons of Jupiter, there were too many to grasp their exact number.

The day after my meeting with Nomiya was saturated with a peculiarly tranquil kind of time. The truffle dog stuck by Agatha's side like her shadow, so there was no need to divide up the hours of my day with him in mind. It was as though I'd been handed a brand-new form of time, a whole and united time, and part of me didn't know what to do with it. Sitting at my desk by the window and staring at my unfinished manuscript, I attempted to drag words out of the void that filled my head. My gaze would drift from the lines of words on the page to what lay beyond the window, settling on the scrap of forest outside. Bathed in the sunlight, the green took on a glassy luster, and the pools of light wavered as they shifted around. The movement of the wind; the minor shifts in the sun's position—with each change of the light, the expression of the forest also altered. When the pattern of the veins standing out on the translucent green came together in my vision with my images of stained glass, the forest began to morph. The trees became pillars holding up a ceiling towering above, and the forest seemed to resemble a gothic church. Then my gaze sank once again into the imaginarium of the greenery.

Reuniting with Nomiya had sent me off into new explorations of my memories. In dreams the previous night, I'd experienced March vicariously. As I made my way from one dreamscape to another, the shreds of my memory tugged at various parts of my body, and each time I woke and was brought back to where I was by the smell of my room or the feel of the bed when I turned in it, I felt utterly disconcerted. The time lag between my memories and the present was like distortions in a bit of glass that had warped inside me.

My fingers remained motionless on the keyboard, enraptured by the smooth feel of the letters on my skin. Only my fingertips retained any sense of reality—the rest of me felt as languid as if it had evaporated into the air. I glanced back at the screen to see I had a message. *Come at 3:00 p.m. on Thursday.* It was a quiet response, reminiscent of Ursula's way of speaking.

I'd come to Göttingen for the second time in March 2017. My first visit had been the year after the tsunami, when I'd studied here for a year. After returning to Japan and finishing my MA, I worked for a while as a teacher in a cram school, while preparing to apply for a PhD. Fortunately, the professor who had taught me while I'd been in Göttingen the first time was still at the university, and it was surprisingly easy to be accepted into their program. In total, it took a year and a half for me to attend language school, pass the required German language exam, and be accepted into the Göttingen University Art History faculty as a doctorate student. I'd been in the city ever since, working on my thesis.

Something I'd been keenly aware of since beginning to put down tentative roots in Göttingen was the stability of the land here, which never shook or trembled. Bodies like mine that are used to living in Tohoku can very quickly detect slight vibrations in the earth's surface. Our sensitivity to tremors was heightened by the earthquake nine years ago, but even before that, we had no choice but to be accustomed to the constant vibration of the earth beneath our feet. After the enormous earthquake, this was honed into a bilayered awareness, composed of two contradictory sensations. We responded sensitively to the small tremors, while simultaneously playing down their significance within our bodies, our consciousnesses. When a two or three magnitude quake would strike in the middle of the night, we'd sit up from our sleep, register what was happening, then quickly return to our sleep and our dreams.

Every time I walked around this German city, I would end up thinking about this profound trust in the earth's surface. It was a lot like the sincerity of a child, viewing their parents with unquestioning faith, truly believing that they were on their side. Entering a shop selling ceramics or wine, I would look at the rows of shelves lining the walls, the bottles and containers stacked there. It was an aesthetic based upon stability. With no provisions in place to prevent them from falling, they were arranged for maximum visual effect, like the objects in a still-life painting. Sustained by this painterly balance, the bottles smiled seductively.

You have an unfailing trust in the earth—I'd murmured these words once to Agatha. A trust in the earth? she'd repeated, with a quizzical expression. We were on the way back from the station, where we'd seen off a friend of hers who'd been visiting from Hamburg. The truffle dog in tow, we passed from the station to Goethe-Allee, making our way along the Planetenweg. It was just as we were passing the bronze post for Earth that I'd said this, and, misunderstanding my "Erde" as referring to the bronze planet, she'd shot a glance in its direction.

There were almost never earthquakes in this country. The only one Agatha had experienced was the one in 1992, whose epicenter was in Roermond in the Netherlands. At a magnitude of 5.4, the earthquake's tremors had been felt across the border in Germany. In some places, the walls of old buildings had collapsed, and tiles fell from roofs; I'd also heard that the cathedrals in Cologne and Aachen had been damaged. This was some thirty years ago, and Agatha had apparently slept right through it. At breakfast, her mother had told her about the earthquake that had happened a little past three in the morning, and five-year-old Agatha had been very aggrieved to have missed out on experiencing it. Since then, she hadn't encountered any other earthquakes.

The untrembling earth quietly accommodated the traditional wooden-framed houses that were dotted around Göttingen like great trees. Those houses were like intricately carved wooden ornaments, in which the sagging of time was visibly recognizable. The pillars and vertical lines in the walls leaned, their ends connected instead by curved lines, swelling out from within so they assumed the shape of loaves of bread—the houses were still steeped in the smells and signs of inhabitation. Through the clouded glass, their windows were by now so warped that they'd grown difficult to open, offering languorous glimpses of the movements of those inside. However misshapen they might become, though, their perpendicularity with the ground was assured—it was clear that both the houses and their inhabitants stood with terrestrial certainty.

And yet, I was still unable to embrace that kind of trust. Holding onto the sensation of the earthquake's tremors that was inscribed within my body, I'd attempted to listen to the ground beneath me, an act that resembled straining my ears. The rhythm of the tremors clung not only to my body but traced the lines of my nerves as well. This was a sensation that would never take root in those who were used to standing on stable ground—of that, too, I felt certain.

This uneasy relationship with the ground beneath me would unexpectedly reveal itself in other ways as well.

As I began going over to Ursula's regularly, I grew familiar with the faces of her other Thursday visitors. Among them was Agnes, a girl of around twelve. She lived with her mother, Barbara, in one of the apartments across the courtyard. At first she'd started coming to Ursula's with her mother, but had subsequently slipped free from her mother's grasp and now came of her own accord, ascending to the rank of a Thursdayer in her own right. Ursula altered neither her tone of voice nor her behavior when interacting with children, yet, with the acuity peculiar to children, Agnes had perceived Ursula's dependability as a listener. Behind their closeness, you could sense a sticky sort of neediness in Agnes, but she never overstepped the boundaries. She never showed up at Ursula's outside of the stipulated time on Thursday.

The way Agnes maintained her distance from others had a lot to do with her anxious nature. And it was only after first sheltering in the shadow of her cautiousness, while carefully and silently observing the other party, that she would attempt to narrow this distance with words. She understood the gap that existed between the Thursdayers and herself, but sometimes she would intentionally ignore it, or cleverly use it to her advantage. After a certain point, she started to loosen up with me, but beneath her apparent amicability lurked a sharp curiosity. I appreciated her honesty, but also couldn't trust her unconditionally. I knew how that kind of forthrightness could become a needle that pierced people as she was speaking to them, without her awareness. In her case, that needle had been stitched inside a particular amusing anecdote. When Agnes found out that I was from Japan, she'd unleashed this treasured story of hers, her trembling lips forming a sniggering, catlike grin.

Last summer, Agnes had gone with a school friend to buy ice cream from a large cafe overlooking the square where the former city hall stood. The ice cream shop was busy in summer, and a snaking line of people would form in front of its doors. Directly in front of Agnes and her friend stood a young couple: a German man and a Japanese woman. The pair stuck their heads out from the line to look at the palette-like array of multicolored ice cream flavors in the window. "What's your favorite flavor?" the man asked the woman. "I like earthquake flavor." A moment later, a burst of laughter flew out of the man's mouth. "Strawberry, you mean strawberry," he corrected her. "Wow, Japanese people sure eat weird stuff." At this, she too began to laugh, slapping him gently on the shoulder. In German, Erdbeeren (strawberries) and Erdbeben (earthquakes)—which both took their beginnings from the word "Erd(e)" meaning "Earth"—were sufficiently similar, so their sounds got mixed up sometimes, in both the memory and the mouth. This earthquake-flavored ice cream story was guaranteed to provoke laughter, and was one of Agnes's favorite anecdotes. That mix-up of words didn't leave any kind of bad taste in her mouth, which explained why for a while, she retold the story over and over, like a party trick. And when I was present, she'd always ask me the same question: "Do you like earthquake flavor, too?" Seeing her face dusted with laughter like cake crumbs, I could only shrug in reply. It didn't matter, she wasn't particularly interested in my response anyway. The story was perfectly shaped as it was, and the question she asked me afterward was only a kind of flourish. The fact that my hometown had been damaged by a recent earthquake, the fact that most Japanese people had earthquakes sensorially inscribed into their bodies—these visceral realities were too remote for her to gauge their distance. If I were to tell these people living in a place where "earthquake" was only an abstract word that I still carried the physical sensations of a far-off land within me, would my comment not be dismissed as outlandish and promptly forgotten about?

Yet the distance between words and embodied experiences whirled and eddied inside me, too. My images of words like "war," "air raid," and "volcanic eruption" weren't accompanied by any physical sensations. I felt an emotional connection with the word "tsunami," yet ultimately I'd never seen one in real life. Quite possibly, to those who lived with that word carved into their bodies, who'd seen that wall of water before their eyes, this connection of mine would seem like a sentimental miscalculation of emotional distance on my part. I couldn't shake the feeling that as my body and my senses acclimatized to this earthquake-free country, that word was losing its heft for me, too. Every time I read an article online about Japan's earthquakes, typhoons, or heavy rains, that suspicion would lodge itself further within me. I suspected that on the underside of this particular emotion lay all my memories of that March day, the places that stayed with me even now, and the sensations I attached to certain words, which I worried constituted a betrayal of Nomiya.

When I climbed the stairs to Ursula's apartment on Thursday afternoon, I found Agnes leaning against the wall of the landing, staring at her phone. Hearing my footsteps, she raised her head, passed a disinterested gaze over me, and said hello. Before I'd even returned her greeting, her eyes had been pulled back to the small screen. Her long, pale hair was puffed up with air, like a little cloud with the sun trapped inside it, and from underneath peeped her small shell-like ears with earphones wedged inside. I guessed those shells must be awash with music, because her body was swaying rhythmically. Determined not to be dragged into that shaking movement, I turned away from the landing and just as I resumed climbing the stairs, she spoke. "Hey," she said, in a somewhat automaton voice. "My mom's still in there, so maybe it's better to wait outside for a bit. They're talking about something important." I turned around and as I was stepping toward her, she lowered her narrow eyebrows fastidiously, as if to say, stop right there. When I sat down on the third stair, still maintaining a distance between us, she smiled, apparently reassured.

Since the spread of the coronavirus, Agnes's anxiety had grown even more severe. She was reluctant to go and see friends, keeping a greater distance between herself and others. Several months had elapsed since the first lockdown, with restrictions on the flow of people and things starting to loosen, and people's feelings grew less constrained as well. Accordingly, there'd been a mass outbreak in June. The mask-wearing requirements for minors weren't as strict as for adults, and when they were outside, most children left their moving mouths unmasked, not paying much attention to the distance they were maintaining—or not maintaining—from others. Agnes, on the other hand, regarded the uncomplicated openness of those around her with suspicion. Her suspicion meant maintaining a safe distance from others, but also included the gazes of other people upon her. She had bad asthma and had endured several unpleasant experiences as a result. Sometimes, during an attack, people had cast sharp, pointed glances in her direction. Eventually, Agnes had come to return the same combative looks back at those around her. To her, uncomplicatedness was now something that could be found in the distance offered by phone and computer screens. There, she could speak with friends in comfort. Looking at her fingers making minute movements across the screen, I addressed her.

"Do you not need to speak to Ursula today?"

"It's my mom who has the appointment. I just came to eat cake."

I felt slightly surprised by these words, displaying a sense of closeness to Ursula that remained unaltered by all that was happening. I wondered if, during this phase that demanded a very grown-up type of endurance and patience, the still potent childlike aspects of Agnes needed Ursula's ears, Ursula's silence, on a material, physical level. By the looks of things, that reliability extended to Ursula's house, which had become a part of Agnes's safe zone.

There was the sound of the door opening, and Barbara appeared, calling Agnes's name. Barbara worked at the library, and often brought books for Ursula. With Agnes standing there watching, we couldn't hug one another in greeting as we had before. "You forgot this," Barbara said, handing her daughter a mask. Shrugging, Agnes put her phone in her pocket. She put on the pale-pink mask with lambs at its four corners, while Barbara donned a red one with a geometric pattern reminiscent of lightning bolts. Looking at their faces with just their foreheads, eyes, and the tops of their noses exposed, it struck me for the first time how alike the mother and daughter were.

Every shelf in Ursula's apartment was crammed full of books, and everything else inside her home gradually assumed a bookish smell. Those books that didn't fit onto the shelves found their own places to be, as though they were cats, hiding out in unexpected locations—under the cushions, behind the row of tea tins, beneath the photo frames. The place was tidy enough, except that the books moved around just as they wished.

The harrowing July heat didn't seem to penetrate the apartment. There was a lot of shade in the north-facing room, where her visitors sat, and the trees in the courtyard helped generate a breeze. It was my first time seeing Ursula in person for four months, but she didn't behave any different now, and only checked to make sure there were no books under the cushion before offering me a seat. Her hair dyed to the shade of a roast chestnut, her petite frame that moved about busily as if keeping rhythm.

On the table sat the usual cheesecake. As I looked at its cocoa powder–dusted surface, I saw a murky image forming there: the marbling created by the brown particles looked bizarrely similar to the surface of Jupiter. A large wedge had been cut from the cake, so it was no longer a perfect circle, but its patterning nonetheless overlapped with the swirls and bands formed by Jupiter's atmosphere. Only one part of the Great Red Spot remained, the rest had been eaten by Agnes. She must've eaten about three slices, Ursula said laughing as she moved a large slice onto a fresh plate. With this new incursion of the knife, the Great Red Spot was erased without a trace from the surface of the cake.

"Speaking of which ..."

Ursula's voice reached my ears a little late, as if from a distance. I noticed that she'd moved around the table and picked up a cup with a swirl of bright blue on it. Her seat was far from the window, engulfed by blue-white shadow. The far-off outside light rendered her face indeterminate, an image reflected on water. As I watched the vague contours of her mouth, it formed the shape of a phrase. The words "grocery shopping" came flying at me, stirring up memories from the previous three months. Finally adjusting to the look of Ursula's face, I was able to turn my attention to her words. She was talking about the middle of March, when there had been various shortages. With gaping holes in the supermarket shelves, there'd been a lot of public distress about the imbalances created by panic buying. Ursula, who'd just returned from a trip to Milan, had been forced to stay at home and quarantine for two weeks, and the Thursdayers had done her shopping for her. I'd made a trip to the supermarket for her, as well. Because of the limitations on the number of people allowed indoors, there was always a neatly spaced line of people outside the shop. Recalling this, the other memories that had been submerged in my body began to rise up. The length of the line. Contact and distance. Welcome warmth and searing cold. My words, directed at Ursula as she prepared the tea—directed at her silence—began twitching. During that March when the virus had been spreading, my body had also been remembering the fragments of that March nine years ago.

Ursula's silence was like a hooked finger, drawing out the memories from inside me.

Four days after the tsunami, when every scrap of food that could be obtained from the local supermarket had run out, I decided to travel into the city. There was a gasoline shortage, so I'd taken public transport instead. I'd set out, intending to take the usual route by bus and train, but with major damage to some of the stations, I had to transfer midway to a replacement bus headed into the town center. The city was surprisingly quiet. The oppressiveness of that silence made time feel as though it had stopped entirely. Time had become a vacuum. The absence of sound halved the presence of the place, and it was redolent with a sense of instability, as if its shadow, as if a crucial part of its body had been wrenched away.

I tagged along with a group of people walking around, trying to find a place to buy food. In the basement of a department store we found a serpentine line of people with the same aim stretching to several hundred meters. We positioned ourselves at its tail, then watched the tail growing ever longer. The snake was so long that no matter how much we waited, we couldn't seem to reach its head. I stomped the ground continuously, the numbness in my fingers growing so severe that I had to bite on my gloves, trying to bring back the sensation in them. With no electricity, there was nowhere to escape the cold. Over the course of a few days, the cold had spun a web throughout my body, and was now so tightly woven that I had no way of loosening the stiffness it caused. Standing in line, my ears began to collect scraps of conversation—how things were in the direction of the sea, on the east side behind the station, in the coastal regions.

Even then, I wasn't thinking of Nomiya at all. It wasn't until a little later that I was able to connect him to the news of the tsunami that had engulfed the coastal region.

A week after the earthquake, I made my way into the research faculty at my university for the first time. Students who'd come from outside the prefecture had mostly gone back to their family homes when it was possible to evacuate, so it was those students living locally, but whose families and houses had escaped the destruction, who showed up to clear up the faculty. Those living by the coast didn't make an appearance for a while longer.

Clearing up the faculty was slow work. Catalogs, collected volumes of essays, and other heavy tomes were strewn across the floor, and the portable bookcases were broken. The impact of falling had damaged some of the older books. As we performed the repetitive task of gathering up books and finding a temporary place of shelter for them in another classroom, we exchanged information with one another about the nuclear power plant and the tsunami victims. We spoke, too, about where we'd been on that day, what we'd been doing at the time, what we'd done afterward, listening closely to what the others told us. This was different from the kind of information that was being exchanged about the coastal regions, whose purpose was to establish the safety or otherwise of those who remained untraceable. We shared an anxiety about the still-ongoing situation, and a strange frothing of emotion that we couldn't contain within ourselves. It was as though we'd come here to perform this manual task in order to find a way to put these things into words. We'd seen the state of the coastal region as it was depicted in photographs in the papers, but between those images and the unknown, a thick, clear distance still intervened. Their irreality was most likely a product of the uncertainty of being so far away, of not having seen the coastal region with our own eyes. Gazing at other people's testimonies and stories that we'd collected, as if turning multifaceted crystals about in our hands, we were perhaps attempting to begin processing what had happened.

Yet when the news that Nomiya was unreachable began to appear in the mouths of the assistants and the teaching staff, accompanied by panicked urgency, our words quietly receded again, our voices were swallowed up by a silence, a silence whose placid surface held not so much as a ripple. News about the damage in Ishinomaki was passed along by word of mouth, but unlike the news about the coastal region in the neighboring prefecture or the designated evacuation zone around the nuclear power plant, which was broad and took the form of a sweeping overview, here, among us, the focus was on the area where Nomiya had lived. I got into the habit of surreptitiously passing my eyes down lists of those in evacuation centers and lists of those who had died that I found online or in the papers. Confronting the names of the dead, in particular, was something that I did when I was alone. Everyone was afraid to look at them, and then experienced guilt after having done so. In the presence of others, we adopted the attitude that Nomiya had survived, but in private, that certainty would be swept away, and we traced the words "dead" and "missing." We had to prepare ourselves for our hopes to be dashed. The names of all those unknown victims I came across whenever I passed my eyes down the list of the dead didn't remain simply as names, rather, they were imbued with the details of lives and temporal experiences I had no way of visualizing, overlaying themselves with the image of the sea that came crashing in from the far side of severed time, they became distant voices ringing out around me. March came to an end, and when the cruel month of April arrived, everyone began to accept that Nomiya had disappeared into the sea.

Since coming to Göttingen, I hadn't spoken in any depth about my memories of the earthquake that had struck so far away from here. Here, the place names belonging to Tohoku—whose land was enveloped in green, whose four seasons were so clearly delineated—were far-flung sounds that slipped right through everyone's ears. If I mentioned the earthquake and the tsunami to someone I was speaking to, their expression would mostly remain foggy. But when I explained that there'd been a nuclear power plant in the area that fog would instantly clear, and they would nod. In their internal maps, the place where I'd been lay vertically adjacent to the focal point—like the moon, orbiting the earth. That place name that symbolized the location of the nuclear reactor had come to haunt and possess their impression of the region in its entirety.

But now Nomiya's arrival had made it impossible for me to gauge my distance from my memories. I struggled to find the words that connected his appearance in this new setting to everything back there—now, since he was so far from the sea into which he'd disappeared, a place where he had neither family or a place to call home. I supposed that I'd still not caught up with the time lag in my memories.

On a whim I decided to ask Ursula, who was making a fresh pot of tea, about the quake that Agatha had missed out on experiencing. "Do you remember the Roermond earthquake?" Ursula halted her movements and narrowed her eyes as she rifled through her memories like someone gazing at the spines of books on the bookshelf. Taking her time, she recalled the 1992 earthquake: she'd been in Göttingen at the time, and felt the earth trembling before dawn. It was clear, however, that the experience hadn't left so much as a scratch in her memory. Her anecdote about the quake was supremely concise, she simply described the momentarily physical sensation as "trembling like a vanilla pudding." The earthquake before that one, with its epicenter in Düren, had been back in the mid-eighteenth century. The temporal distance between the present and an earthquake over two hundred years ago was sufficiently large that the occurrence had been tidied away, seen as an anomalous historical event. The discrepancy in Ursula's and my familiarity levels on the subject meant the thread of our conversation grew tangled, and I started to feel hesitant when speaking to Ursula about the events of the past leading back from Nomiya's arrival.

By the time I left Ursula's apartment, there was a half-formed heaviness in my stomach, precipitated not just by the cake I'd eaten, but also the words I'd been unable to say. Ultimately, I hadn't managed to speak into the silence Ursula provided of Nomiya's arrival, or the memories it had brought to the surface. My memories may have been unspooling, but when I went to voice them, they coiled themselves around my tongue and refused to emerge. The words Ursula had said when I'd left had lodged in my ears: *The past always borrows a face, a likeness. If the face is blurry, you have to take time to remember it.* In my head I clawed away at that white, faceless mask, like one of the dancers in the sculpture, but it spun and slipped through my fingers, refusing to reveal its features to me.

When I stepped from the apartment building into the courtyard, the sunlight was pouring through the trees, with their glistening leaves hanging down heavily. Hushed laughter wove its way through the foliage into my ears. I felt sure it must belong to Agnes, but I couldn't see any trace of her—I could only hear the laughing of the trees. With these half-formed reminiscences, I felt myself becoming a ghostlike presence, out of place from my surroundings. I decided to go somewhere quiet, to try to rid myself of this dissatisfaction.

St. Jacobi-Kirche was roughly equidistant from Ursula's apartment and the Jupiter post. If your lowered your eyes to the cobbles out the front of the church, you found them dotted with bronze tiles, on whose surface the figure of a golden scallop rose up from a black background. The scallop was both the pilgrim's symbol and St. Jacobi's attribute. In German, scallop is Jakobsmuschel—St. Jacobi's shell, with St. Jacobi being the German name for St. James. The inextricable connection between the shell and the saint was evident both verbally and visually. If an icon wore a hat with a shell on it, you would instantly know it was St. James. This was a pictorial realm where the individual was identified not through their features or their bodily form, but through their attributes.

St. Jacobi-Kirche was known as a pilgrimage church. Named for the saint that guides those on their travels, it had been built beside the road as a place of rest for travelers. In the Middle Ages, a pilgrimage was a lifelong journey, and pilgrimage destinations included Spain's Santiago de Compostela, as well as Rome and Jerusalem. The Way of St. James that crossed through France and into Spain also worked its way through Germany like a network of blood vessels. Göttingen lay on the route that led down from the Scandinavian nations, one of the stops along the scallop shell trail alongside Lübeck and Hanover. The pilgrimage leading to the destination where St. James's remains lie is still undertaken to this day. Pilgrims on the trail had once carried the scallop shells that symbolized St. James to identify themselves.

Stepping inside the church, built between the fourteenth and fifteenth centuries, my eyes and my ears were dragged into its quietude. Since visiting this church numerous times, I'd come to know that its silence had the texture of water. There was no excessive decoration on the ceilings or walls, which were subsumed by a comparatively quiet white. Rows of columns led like a grove of trees to the altar, their bark imprinted with a unique pattern. Intertwining gray and red diamonds climbed up the surface of the columns toward the heavens. This geometrical pattern dated back to the fifteenth century, when the law of perspective had first been discovered. If you traced the surface of the columns beside you, the pattern befuddled your perspective of the space. The two-tone patterning that enveloped the column like lizard scales was different on each column, growing fatter and thinner in turn, using illusion to enhance the sense of the space's depth.

Perspective creates depth and distance in paintings and spaces: the ceiling of the church's Gothic interior seemed to stretch up endlessly. A simple drawing depicting the coastline, with all that lay inside shrouded in white, rose up on the surface of my eyelids. Was that what lay beyond the vanishing point here? Perspective also played a role within memory. The image positioned as the focal point altered how the other memories were arranged within one's own personal map. Time introduced assorted vanishing points to the arrangement, which enabled one to inspect the memory freely. And yet for us, our sole internal vanishing point was set, inexorably, as that March day.

Now the perspective of time placed a focus on even more distant memories. I'd first begun conversing with Nomiya because he'd shown an interest in German art. At that point, I'd been a first-year MA student. One day, in the Western Art History faculty, Nomiya asked for my advice on the subject he should choose for his final-year dissertation. With the academic year having ended in February, it was the time when the undergrads who would become fourth years in April were starting to mull over their research topics.

German art wasn't a popular field. In the world of art history research, Teutonic art from bygone eras proved an unfashionable choice. Its lurid color contrasts, grotesquely exaggerated facial expressions, and awkward physicalities meant that most were unable to perceive its beauty. It veered away from any harmonious ideal, and its extremity sometimes made one flinch.

In general, students would gradually come to sense within themselves an orientation toward a certain part of Europe from within the artists and artworks that they encountered through their seminars and assignments. Nomiya had been researching Andrea del Sarto—a sixteenth century Italian artist—and his circle, whose style had been influenced by Leonardo da Vinci: that gentle, listless touch that one found in religious paintings; the light that looked as though it had passed through unfathomable stretches of time before arriving at its current location. Nomiya's first point of contact with Andrea del Sarto came from a mention of him in Natsume Soseki's *I am a Cat*, where Waverhouse's advice to Professor Sneaze to sketch from nature is erroneously attributed to the artist. Following this advice at face value, Professor Sneaze undertakes a life drawing of a cat as an experiment. When I asked Nomiya why he'd then decided to cross the Alps, he replied that a picture he'd seen in a German museum had left a big impression on him. The lines he traced with his finger across the large desks of the faculty were also those that led him to a certain painter.

During the summer break of 2010, Nomiya went on a trip that led him to visit the art museums of the UK, Italy, and Germany. He gazed at the paintings Soseki had praised in London's National Gallery, completely exhausted both his feet and his eyes in Italy's churches and art museums, before winding up in Munich. There, in the Alte Pinakothek, he encountered a group of paintings whose portrayal of the sky and the surrounding scenery struck him as exceptional. The artist was Albrecht Altdorfer, an early sixteenth-century painter from Regensburg, Bavaria—one of the pioneers of unadulterated landscape painting at a time when nature and landscape were regarded as secondary, background subjects, who liberally used forms of expression that saw the natural scenery leavened with the world of the imagination. This different way of looking at landscapes extended also to the depiction of astronomical phenomena and the weather. With his brush, the earth and the sky above it burst free from their shell of symbolism, becoming no longer simply intimations of the worlds of the gods.

Nomiya was particularly captivated by Altdorfer's depictions of astronomical phenomena and light sources in the sky. In his version of the Nativity scene, the star of Bethlehem assumed a unique shape, reminiscent of a fireball. This sparked Nomiya's interest in the conception and illustration of the cosmos at this time. At that point in history, nature was viewed through the filter of two distinct types of mystery. Religious understanding began to come together with the observational perspective, and divinity could now be found within nature itself.

Yet when I asked Nomiya if he planned to research Altdorfer's religious paintings for his dissertation, he promptly shook his head. I want to write about *The Battle of Alexander at Issus*, he said.

The painting in question was Altdorfer's depiction of a battle that took place in 333 BC. Its subject matter is, ostensibly, a historical event where Alexander the Great's Macedonian troops defeated the Persians, yet it was also important as a landscape painting. This scene of the vast conflict rendered in colorful waves subsuming the foreground is that of regulated chaos. Rather than centralizing any specific heroic figure, the image is focused on the locale, the occasion. Yet what specifically attracts the viewer's gaze is the sea and the sky spreading out at the back of the canvas. In contrast to the dynamic colors of the foreground, the blue-steeped mountain range is sunken in quietude, as though it had closed its eyes meditatively, patiently waiting for night to fall. The Mediterranean Sea stretched horizontally along the canvas reflects the movements of the sky, its surface tinged with touches of crimson and white alongside a profusion of blues. To the West, the sun sinks into the horizon, while high on the opposite side of the sky, the crescent moon representing the East twinkles faintly, a translucent white. The movement of the voluminous clouds encircling the wooden plaque that floats in the center of the sky appears ominous, but with the power to lift the eye perpetually upward, to the highest heights. The fluid movement rolling from deep to mid blue; a perspective reminiscent of a bird's, surveying the earth from above while facing the sky.

When Nomiya saw this interplay of colors on the canvas, it came together in his mind with the sea that he'd observed for so long, and the landscape to which it belonged. Living as he did by the sea in Ishinomaki, the tonal shifts in color and expression that played out across the sky and sea were incredibly familiar to him. The sensations and memories that had built up in him over time invoked a shared sensibility with the work of this artist, who was separated from him both temporally and geographically.

As Nomiya slowly described this vision of the sea to me, I felt it being absorbed by all the associations for blue that I'd accumulated over the years, sinking right into their deepest stratum, as though a piece of blue glass had been implanted inside me. That depiction of the sea and the sky that reflected the weather, the seasons, and the time of day must have originated out of a pellucid, meticulously observant gaze. The sensory experiences and the shared language of those accustomed to living near the sea spilled out across the image of that old painting in the catalog, which was spread open in front of us, resonating in my ears like the tales of some far-off place. These were the words of someone who had beheld with their own eyes a blue that could be traced all the way back to a sixteenth-century painting.

That was the last conversation that I had with Nomiya in the university. Less than two weeks later, he was swallowed up by the sea.

After succumbing to the floating sensation engendered by the perspective in the church, I went to look at the main altarpiece. The three-layered altarpiece consisted of a panel depicting the life of St. James, for whom the church was named, a scene illustrating Jesus's life and crucifixion, and a gilded wood carving of Christ with the saints. The panels were displayed in rotation according to the liturgical season. On most of my visits, however, I would encounter the life of Christ panel. The light seeping through the stained glass windows softly unfolded the colors of those episodes rendered against a golden background, so the suffering and death pervading the scenes of the latter half of Christ's life seemed somehow far removed. His crucifixion wasn't the last sequence of the scenes—these were of his burial and resurrection from the tomb. I attempted to superimpose Nomiya's story onto the scenes of the panel. In my imagination, the scene of his death was only ever a great mass of sea. His body still hadn't been found, yet here he was in Göttingen. I supposed that wasn't something comparable, something that could be conflated with the images of the resurrection.

The third panel, which I'd only seen a few times, was composed of the Virgin Mother and child along with sixteen saints. The saints weren't crowded into the middle of the panel, like some sort of group photo, but rather formed a long line, with Christ and the Virgin Mary in the center. The canopies, columns, and other intricately depicted architectural features ensured a sense of distance between the saints. Four of the saints were women, cloaked in golden robes with touches of pink on their cheeks and gentle smiles on their faces. Noting their attributes, I rummaged around in my mind for their names. There was St. Elizabeth of Thuringia, holding a bread basket, and St. Catherine of Alexandria grasping a wheel and sword, wearing a crown. The one with the container of ointment was Mary Magdalene, and the other one holding the small basket was St. Dorothea. It was far easier to determine their characteristics and identities than those other saints who asserted their authority by ostentatiously brandishing books and staffs.

The subject of my doctorate thesis was the evolution in the representations of the Fourteen Holy Helpers in Germany from the Middle Ages onward, and how this intersected with religious faith. Originally a Roman Catholic concept, the imagery of the Fourteen Holy Helpers provides an example of the reverence for saints that spread through Germanic nations between the fifteenth and early sixteenth centuries. These images are found all across Europe, but each region has certain saints that they are more strongly affiliated with. In particular, a place name appears in a saint's nomenclature indicates a solid connection to that specific region. This group of fourteen saints was believed to aid in averting sudden death from sickness and pain, accidents and so on. Death and suffering could worm their way into human life in myriad ways, appearing unexpectedly and leaving one little choice but to live in close quarters with them. In their attempt to keep them at arm's length for as long as possible, people dedicated their prayers to those saints who'd undergone torture and death of a kind related to their own suffering. These saints were experts in the type of suffering that was inscribed into the body, and therefore, it was thought, could protect people from sickness and death.

The Christian saints were numerous, and when depicted figuratively, they always had the same visual attributes and symbols, by which they could be identified. Books, staffs, keys, jars, lambs, and so on—their attributes were deeply connected to the narratives associated with them. For that reason, many of the martyred saints carried the instruments of their torture or their afflicted body parts. These externalized symbols of pain served as the means of their identification—the tools of their pain enabled them to be distinguished from other saints; their severed body parts allowed them to be recognized. Guided by these symbols, those seeking help would pray to them to be healed from sickness, released from threat of death. St. Barbara held in her hand the tower where she'd been confined, St. Sebastian was pictured with his body riddled with arrows, St. Apollonia held a set of forceps with a tooth inside—all seeming to suggest that suffering was a way of creating a recognizable identity for oneself.

Two that stood out as particularly bizarre in this regard were St. Lucia of Syracuse and St. Agatha of Sicily. The former had had her eyes gouged out and the latter her breasts torn off, both as forms of torture. When they appeared in paintings, the women modestly held up the severed parts of their bodies. St. Lucia's attribute is her eyes. She is depicted with two beautiful eyes, while also carrying, in her hands or on a plate, two more eyes, complete with eyelids and eyelashes. I would find myself wondering: which pair is really hers? The same question could be directed at St. Agatha. To reflect the fact that her breasts had been lopped off, she too holds up a plate with two rounded breasts perched atop it like desserts. In St. Agatha's case, her clothing obscures her chest, so it's unclear whether or not there is another pair of breasts concealed underneath. Did these duplicate body parts not strike the women as surplus to requirements? My scholarly interest was particularly focused on how these severed body parts coexisted with the saints' intact bodies, and how the saints continued to carry them around even after their deaths, as fragments of their agonizing memories.

A mental memory was sustained by a physical one. Repetition inscribed those physical memories even deeper into the body, like bruises.

The memories of that March day weren't confined to the visual realm. I was almost certain that the sense of the catastrophe was imprinted into every part of my body. My right hand: the feel of the dog's back trembling in fear during the aftershocks; the feel of that brittle fur that had lost its former sheen, which I stroked all those nights that I couldn't sleep; the unconscious habit of flicking the light switch in the middle of the night, and the ensuing disappointment when nothing happened. My left hand: the red markings to my skin and the pain as the plastic bag that contained food that I'd waited in line for so long to buy, cutting into my flesh; the cold ache that ran through my fingertips as I swept up the bits of broken dishes; the cold and wet of the water flowing out the only tap in the local community center, the only place that still had running water, by which I'd stood in line to fill up a plastic bottle. My ears: the sense of absence on the roads, no longer being used by cars; the conversations of people trying to piece together bits of information; the sound of the radio; the sound of various voices on the other end of the phone when I finally got through to someone I'd been trying to contact; the screech-like meowing of the starving cat living on the university campus as it came running up to me; the sound of it chewing when I gave it canned or dried cat food. My feet: the arrhythmic stomping driven by hunger and cold in the long line to buy food; the feel of the soles of my feet grown hard after walking everywhere in the absence of buses. My stomach: the painful hunger; the way that part of my digestive system continued to protest even after its starvation had ended. Nose: a heightened sensitivity to food smells; the smell of bodies that stayed indoors all day; the mildewed time contained within old books. Skin: the dirt and sticky weight that accumulates when you can't wash; the cold that pierces like needles.

It isn't just images that become memories. Different parts of my body stored up memories, which they silently retained. Those afterimages carried that way in the body would most likely never be erased. Skin cells regenerate periodically, becoming new, but the time that passed after the earthquake and sensations from that period seemed to linger on, as a transparent layer on my skin. And yet, when I tried to pass beyond my memories, all I could see was a two-dimensional whiteness. Connecting together all my physical memories only left me with a dense accumulation of fragments—I never managed to summon up a complete picture of that day. The attributes of the memories held by each part of my body may have been a part of me, but I couldn't combine them into any self-identifying symbols, like those of the saints. Being in a place so far away from the sea and nuclear power plants had loosened my grip on my memories of that day, obscuring my connection to them.

Coming out of the church, I walked down the Planetenweg toward the Sun, emerging onto a wide road that ran perpendicular between Mars and Jupiter. I often rode my bike along this road, beside the flow of cars. Sometimes I'd be pursued by a bus as I pedaled, but my bike was too small for me to begin with, so it was hard to gain any distance from it. Even when I pumped my legs faster, attempting to keep up with the other bikers around me, they would always be able to smoothly overtake me. When a bus or bike was hemming me in from behind, I would feel like a hunted animal. At certain times of day, the road would become crowded with bikes and cars like an asteroid belt. Venturing through the path of orbit like a small fragment of rock, I would try to concentrate on my own pedaling, as I clung to a chilling vision of the other moving objects crashing into me and sending me flying.

Needing to ignore the close proximity between me and the huge chunks of metal behind me, my senses would grow somewhat warped. After a while, I would sense the contours of my body—everything outside my feet pumping the pedals and my hands gripping the handlebars—dissolving, so I felt as though I were fluttering around in midair. I hadn't been using my bike as much recently, but the sensation of being chased from behind hadn't diminished at all. Maybe the thing chasing me was the memories that Nomiya the ghost had brought with him, and the memories belonging to all the disconnected parts of my body were attempting, uneasily, to rise to the surface.

I hadn't been in touch with Nomiya again, even after visiting Ursula. Instead, I kept making excuses to myself, listing the reasons I had for not meeting with him. If only he'd gone to a different city—every time this wistful thought crossed my mind I'd be seized by guilt, peeling off the skin of my emotions, little by little. He hadn't been in touch with me either, and as a result his presence wasn't actually impacting my life in any way.

Less than two weeks after Nomiya's arrival, odd rumors began circulating through the city. The bronze post for Pluto had started to appear at the end of the Planetenweg, which now ended with Neptune. Back when the Planetenweg was first installed in 2003, there'd been a bronze post for Pluto, next to the tower named for Otto von Bismarck, which lay in the forest southeast of Neptune. Then in 2006, Pluto—formerly considered the ninth planet in the solar system—had been relegated from the category of planet, and deemed instead a dwarf planet. This heralded a change to the Planetenweg in Göttingen, with the Pluto bronze post being removed. In 2013, the post was replaced by a plaque commemorating the Gaussian unit system, invented by the mathematician Carl Friedrich Gauss. Two years later, a new bronze post representing Pluto as dwarf planet was stationed outside of the Max Planck Research Institute in the north of the city.

Nobody understood the significance of this return of the old Pluto post, although there was plenty of speculation and chatter. In time, the rumors metamorphosed in strange ways, much like birds that have lost their sense of direction and go crashing into glass windows. Perhaps because people had been cooped up inside since March, those now with plenty of time on their hands began walking to the Bismarck Tower or the Max Planck Institute to see for themselves whether the rumors about Pluto were, in fact, true. The bronze post symbolizing Pluto as a dwarf planet still stood outside the Institute. This meant that the new post appearing in front of the tower in the woods had to be the original post containing the model of Pluto, from before it'd been taken down. Did this new reappearance express some veiled intent to restore Pluto's full planetary status, or was it, too, a species of nostalgia for bygone days? But either way, the authorities could have simply removed the post, thereby ending the confusion for once and for all.

As it was, the problem lay in the irregularity of the old Pluto's appearance. The bronze post would appear and disappear, across different times and days. It wasn't always positioned beside the tower—instead, it vanished sporadically, like a trick that the forest was playing on its visitors. Yet the numbers of people who'd witnessed the post was increasing. To go by their testimony, as well as the photos and videos shared online, the post wasn't some portable thing that could easily be moved—it was a bronze plaque set in white stone, just like the original, and too well rendered to be a mere replica. For a while, some had suggested that the images showing the post were fake, but since there were new testimonies from people of all ages and backgrounds, this skepticism soon dried up, and the eyewitness accounts assumed greater credibility. As soon as it was widely accepted that the post actually existed, however, its repeated disappearance and reappearance began to seem very odd indeed, and the rumor mill grew even busier.

The word Pluto, stemming from the Latinized form of the Greek "Ploutōn," is the name for the ruler of the underworld—the place where the dead go. The appearance of a planet on the Planetenweg made it seem as if death, which had grown distant, was reassuming its place alongside us. Various impressions and memories flitted through my mind: those who were affected by the deaths that the continuing pandemic was causing; those related to Nomiya who had disappeared into the sea in the catastrophe nine years ago. It was as though the message from the model of what'd once been the ninth planet was none other than a mockingly delivered "memento mori"—remember you must die. As though Pluto itself had become a ghost, rooted once again in its former location.

Then it struck me: the place where Nomiya was staying must've been close to the Max Planck Institute. There were a lot of apartment complexes in this neighborhood, mostly inhabited by natural science students. It was a considerable distance on foot from the old town, and usually required traveling by bus or a bike. With a mountain and a expanse of forestland nearby, the area felt very much on the outskirts of the city. In other words, Nomiya didn't live too far away from the place where the Pluto post was currently positioned.

I hadn't been to visit him in that far-off neighborhood, and it seemed that he mostly stayed at home, perhaps also because of the distance. Yet, around the time I began hearing the strange rumors about Pluto, a message arrived from him: "I saw the truffle dog in Göttingen." My gaze was hooked by the word Göttingen, which was written out in kanji characters: 月沈原.

In the Japanese of the past, rather than using the phonetic katakana alphabet to write the names of foreign places as is done now, each locale was assigned its own kanji exonym, which carried a specific meaning, but also conveyed the way it sounded to the ear. Berlin, for example, was 伯林: "chief" and "grove"; Cologne was 歌倫: "song" and "ethics." Dresden was 徳停: "virtue" and "stop"; Munich was 民顕: "citizens" and "appear." These kanji, chosen because they most closely matched the sounds of the word, changed one's impression of a place in a peculiar way—sometimes delightfully so. Thus for me, Berlin's kanji painted a picture of forests owned by the Margraf—the military governor of the border provinces—which would stage great hunts in fall, and the forests would be dotted by horses that galloped through at the sound of a whistle or the bark of a dog. In the music festival in Cologne, its name indicated, the judging would be carried out on the basis of both musical talent and moral virtue. Then there was Dresden, where monks were plotting a mass escape, and Munich, where a popular movement had caught on and had turned revolutionary. My internal map was colored by the scraps of the narrative that these Japanese place names projected onto it.

In this old schema, Göttingen was written as moon, sink, plain—an open plain into which the moon was sinking. This beautiful, somehow melancholy combination of characters resonated with the Japanese fixations with the moon and with nature. Written in kanji, the name—月沈原—carried within it the power to spirit one away to a far-off location. The row of three quiet letters seemed to me both like a mask that the city had worn, and another face of the city woven into the fabric of time.

Yet those kanji had already become unused and forgotten—why had they appeared here, now, in Nomiya's message? Reading it, my eyes snagged on that unfamiliar nomenclature. The rest of his message was an extremely ordinary summary of what he'd been doing in the city. He asked a question about his visa application procedure, told me that he'd signed up for lessons at a language school, talked about applying to use the university library, and discussed the items he'd bought from the Asian grocery store, all in a tempered style—and nowhere else broaching the subject of Göttingen's past, at least so far as I could see. The meeting with the truffle dog was reported out of the blue, with no mention of the context in which it'd occurred or its relation with anything else, and it was there that the town's name written in kanji made its first appearance. There was no way it could've been a simple inputting error—the notation was too rare for that. I sent a reply, saying how pleased I was that his life in the city seemed to be on track, but I didn't mention the name issue.

Yet the fact that this old nomenclature resurfaced and overlapped temporally with the spectral reappearance of the old Pluto post left me with an odd feeling that I couldn't shake off: as I continued to suspect that the post occurrence was in some way connected with Nomiya's arrival, there were further developments concerning the changes to the forest.

Just when the rumors about the ghostly Pluto post had begun to die down, I heard a strange story from Agatha. She was one of the city's dedicated forest hikers. There were many Göttingen inhabitants who, enticed by the forests sprawling to the north and east and the walking route around the old town that was enveloped in green, found themselves becoming serious nature lovers. The constraints placed upon people's lives since March had created an increase in the number of people who walked regularly for exercise and stress relief. Agatha was in the habit of walking with the truffle dog through the woods as far as the Neptune post, and then turning back. She said that she didn't make it as far as the Bismarck Tower to verify whether or not the Pluto post—the continued subject of the all the rumors—was there. Without going right into the heart of the forest, even by just sticking to its edges, you could still enjoy plenty of silence, she would say with a smile. I sensed that her self-assured pronouncement wasn't unrelated to her expectations concerning the whereabouts of truffles, but I said nothing.

And yet, she'd started to perceive changes along her walking route, too. The truffle dog had begun to show a strange new propensity for collecting things. Now, whenever she took him to the patch of forest near Neptune, he would unearth something or other from the soil. These items weren't truffles or poisonous mushrooms or dead animals. When I asked her what kind of objects had been excavated, Agatha reeled off a list: a cane, a toy sword, a dart, a stuffed sheep, a rusty goblet, a basket with a broken handle, a doll house shaped like a tower. In other words, objects that had evidently belonged to other people before being lost or taken away. But so strange and unlikely were their hidden locations, it was hard to think they had been dropped there accidentally. Agatha, believing their appearance signified a lack of etiquette or respect on the part of the visitors, grew heated as she spoke of illegal dumping. Each time this came up in conversation, the topic would shift from these littered items discovered in the woods to attitudes toward environmental preservation. The truffle dog, who was responsible for discovering these objects, seemed to have lost his olfactory memory of the black, asteroid-like mushrooms. When he turned up these fragments of human lives from within the soil instead, he would present them proudly to his owner. Agatha, infuriated by this evidence of the litter and pollution in the city's green spaces, saved pictures of the items on her smartphone. This process was repeated over and over.

On just one occasion Sawata had spoken with me about what he'd seen by the sea.

Waiting until some time had elapsed since that March day, he decided to travel as close as he could to the coast where Nomiya had been. He found that the objects littering the area had lost their form, lost sight of their original usage, lost any connection to the people who had used them, begun to lose even their names. And even if son.ething had retained its previous shape or appearance, it'd already been left behind by the flow of time. These objects could be recognized by feeling around for their past correspondences, identified as what they *used to be*. Yet on their inside, these objects were brimming with the words that connected them to memories. Dolls, shoes, cars, bags, clothes, books, desks, and chests of drawers— they weren't simple nouns, but fragments of a human past that had been wrenched from time. Sawata saw traces of the people in these things. He didn't personify them, but rather regarded them as proof of past lives, proof of everything that had been stolen from this place. But even in beholding these pieces of some unknown person's voice, even knowing for certain that this voice had belonged to a particular someone, Sawata was unable to share in its memories. Those things swollen with seawater and covered in mud, even the things that were so damaged they were barely intact, Sawata perceived as the visual manifestation of invisible voices that came to reverberate inside him, although he couldn't grasp the meaning of what they were trying to say. However attentively he listened, the most he could conjure up were vague human outlines. And as he pressed forward, he found these words getting swallowed up by the whispers and screams of objects—swallowed up by their silence. Walking around this place, filled with things that had ceased to retain their forms, he realized for the first time just how much objects took on their shape in relation to people, from within people's lives, and from the complexity of the ways in which we registered life and time.

The coastal region and the inner city—going back and forth between those two locations, Sawata's vision began to be possessed by the specters of objects. The mounds of rubble lingered hazily in his sight, still appearing on the back of his eyelids when he shut his eyes to block them out. The images seemed altogether too vivid to be intimations of death—and that was the problem, most likely. For his MA thesis, he'd chosen to write about Nicolas Poussin's *Et in Arcadia ego*. Multiple paintings with this title existed, all of them featuring a skull looking very out of place against a pastoral backdrop. Here was death that comes to look you in the eye, regardless of your location. The paintings were intended to serve as a reminder that death exists even in the idyll of Arcadia.

I recalled Sawata's words as he'd related his experiences to me: "After those scenes from the coast had gotten stuck inside my vision, there was a time when I couldn't bear to look at any Surrealist paintings depicting strange combinations of objects, or objects and places. The clock, twisted out of shape, lying on the beach. The pastoral landscape merging with a room's interior. The bed lying on a beach in winter. The bodies, themselves like objets d'art, formed out of assorted items. I was used to seeing paintings forging links between items that had nothing to do with one another. But the objects that appeared before my eyes weren't enclosed inside a frame like an artwork—they were the reality that lay outside of it. When you saw a ship deposited where a house had once been, or a car that had been carried off by the sea and stacked on top of another car, you couldn't leave those to the realm of Surrealist images or dreams, and escape to a reality where things took on some kind of order. I kept on seeing the gap, almost an unbreachable chasm, that existed between the irreality of pictures and the irreality of reality. I couldn't connect my memories of Nomiya with those things that I saw before my eyes, either, to the point that I felt that those memories had been partially lost."

Eventually, all of those things were cleared away, revealing a landscape where everything had vanished. Even without the objects, though, the voices remained, and that silence in which voices jostled and rubbed up against one another still echoed within the area. The memory fragments that continued to fill Sawata's ears and eyes kept Nomiya's likeness at a distorted distance.

Around the time when the truffle dog was unearthing all kinds of unusual objects, Lucia and Katharina came over for dinner. Now that lockdown had ended, we were able to have small numbers of houseguests inside again. The issue, however, was the apartment itself, which hadn't seen any visitors in a while. Even after a good clean, it seemed to retain a jet-lagged expression. As I rattled around with the noisy vacuum cleaner, Agatha prepared the meal in the kitchen. At the bottom of a pan filled with rested a mound of pasta shells; in a deeper pan, a sauce with chunks of vegetables was bubbling as if taking short, sharp breaths. With her back to the stove, Agatha was carefully removing the tendons from a large joint of meat with a knife. She was pushing down hard with her right arm and shoulder, creating a muffled clunk each time the knife struck the chopping board. That sound alone was sufficient warning to stay out of her way. Hoping to escape the dull, low noise of the chopping, I flung the vacuum cleaner around even more noisily, maintaining my distance from Agatha.

That Saturday evening, as the sky had clouded over and the air finally started to cool, Lucia rang the doorbell. I opened it to find her standing there in an unusual pale-blue polka dot mask, her eyes smiling gently. Lucia worked for an optician. She, too, I'd met at Ursula's house. Through her delicate gold-rimmed glasses, her blue-gray eyes had a transparency like that of late-winter evenings. In Sendai, the sky above the snow-lined ground would sometimes assume this color, but I hadn't seen this exact same color since coming here. The white of the snow wasn't directly reflected in the sky above, but made it impossible to gauge its depth. There was no metallic hardness about this pale blue—rather, it was a soft, hazy shade, with an inner richness. Lucia's eyes made me recall the sweet, cold March air, and the feel of the snow.

Around her neck, she wore an eye-shaped pendant—an eyeball rendered in blue glass. Against a background of artificial midnight blue lay a circle of opaque white glass, its contours indistinct, and on top of that, a black speck of glass like a seed. I felt a tickle in my memory—I knew I'd seen something like this before, but couldn't remember what it was called.

"What is that?"

"It's a *nazar boncuğu*. A Turkish amulet." Unlike the soft expression of Lucia's eyes, this oculus, whose function was to ward off the evil eye and malicious spirits, was a stiff, cold blue that reflected no emotion.

As Lucia moved inside to greet Agatha, Katharina also arrived.

"It's been a while!" she said. Her voice was cheerful, but her lips didn't move much. An MA student in philosophy, Katharina was also the proofreader of my doctoral thesis, which I was writing in German. Her language was like perfectly polished glass, occasionally so precise that it was like a sharp sword piercing me across my entire body. As I directed my gaze at the little wheel-shaped earrings hanging from her lobes, I prayed intently that she wouldn't ask about how my thesis was coming along.

During the meal, our conversation started out along the safest and most easily comprehensible route. Discussing our respective news, various anecdotes, and the federal government's policies, we tried to reconnect our lives, which had been severed from one another for a while now. There was still a strangeness that came from being confronted by everyone's faces like this—not communicating through words or faces across a screen. As we each had our own individual rhythms, we paced the conversation to the tempo of our meal. Yet when we'd finished our main course, and were embarking on the dessert, Agatha broached a new conversation topic, as if serving us fresh plates. It was, of course, the issue of the woods.

"It seems worse the closer you get to the Bismarck Tower. It's all these people caught up in this stupid trend, I'm sure of it," Agatha declared after explaining the truffle dog's discoveries, her tone bright and sharp. At first, both Lucia and Katharina's faces expressed bemusement: they gazed down at the ice cream in their bowls, but eventually they seemed to understand what she was getting at, and smiles twitched at the corners of their mouths. Agatha was critical of people taking selfies without any respect for their surroundings. There'd been a piece in the news about people taking selfies at Auschwitz, and on that subject, too, she had been merciless: "I can't believe that people would use a place like that as a background to take pictures of themselves," she had said. "That place is already a portrait—a portrait of a specific time, of people's memories. How can anyone possibly think of photographing themselves there, when there are already countless faces engraved into that scene?" She also applied that way of seeing things—valuing the portrait-like nature of a place—to the forestland that sprawled out to the east of the city. Now the conversation returned to the forest itself.

"All these people rushing out to the forest because it's trendy all of a sudden just treat it like any other setting."

"But a place is a place, right?"

"All I'm saying is that they only see it as a backdrop. A pathway to their desired destination."

"And you think the forest is the protagonist."

"Yes, exactly. The walkers are just a transient element.

They're so obsessed with selfies that their priorities are all off."

"Of course you'd say that, as someone who loathes selfies."

"But it's true, right? They want to be seen as having a good relationship with nature, and so they're looking at the forests exclusively through the lens of their own ego."

The more she spoke, the more Agatha's wrath spread its wings, allowing its feathers to be ruffled. Spurred on, she pulled up on her phone the photographs she'd been storing up.

Are you sure all this stuff is connected with the people who go to see the Pluto post? Katharina murmured in her silvery tones. These aren't the sorts of things that people carry around with them, are they? At the sound of her calm voice, the discussion of this inflammatory topic seemed to stop escalating. The photo folder on Agatha's phone contained a visual index of the huge variety of items the truffle dog had found. Again and again, she swiped her finger across the screen—there seemed no end to the pictures of all those objects that had been dug up in the soil. The sense of human presence still hung over the objects, which meant that looking at them induced the uncomfortable feeling of examining someone's belongings after their death. "Wait!" The group of us had fallen quiet as we watched the parade of photos, but at the sound of Lucia's sudden cry, we looked up from Agatha's finger sweeping across the screen. When Agatha scrolled back a few shots, to the image Lucia indicated, I saw what looked like a pale-blue flower. When Agatha zoomed in, I realized that it was a *nazar boncuğu* covered in dirt. Its cracked stare was looking intently into Lucia's eyes.

After obtaining a number of photos from Agatha, Lucia decided to leave, her reasons vague. Katharina closely examined the photographs in front of her, but didn't share any of her observations, simply stirring her melted ice cream with her spoon to create a strange marble pattern of pink, white, and green. Just as she was preparing to go, she asked Agatha, hesitantly, if she could send her the photos of the toy wooden sword and the bicycle wheel. It was evident that the objects discovered in the forest had robbed both women of words. Seeing how the events of the evening only seemed to have led us further inside the labyrinth, Agatha appeared to have lost the will to speak about the forest any further. Saturday passed, and even the next day, on Sunday, she didn't head out to the woods beside Neptune.

The following Thursday, Ursula messaged Agatha, asking to see the photos of the things that the truffle dog had dug up in the woods. It seemed evident that either Lucia or Katharina, both regular Thursdayers, must've visited Ursula and told her about the excavations. Agatha cocked her head at the request, but sent the entire folder to Ursula. I discovered later that Ursula's message had also mentioned accompanying Agatha on a walk to Neptune, and collecting some of the objects unearthed by the truffle dog. All of a sudden, Agatha and I found ourselves rendered immobile by a frigid unease about this situation, which seemed to be forcing us to traverse an off-kilter orbit.

Was this all connected in some way with the bronze model of Pluto? As the two of us speculated about the significance of Ursula's request, we avoided discussing that particular issue. Oblivious to our discomfort, the truffle dog continued his tour of the cool spots in the apartment, napping in one before moving onto the next. What exactly was he sniffing out now, instead of the meteorite fungi? Watching his occasionally twitching nose, I thought about the various representations of death that I'd come to associate with Pluto.

As the phase of my orbit was shifting, I once again received a long message from Nomiya. My attention once again drawn by the old notation for Göttingen—月沈原—I let my eyes skim over it:

My lessons at the language school have begun, but they're still mostly online. It felt odd to be on a screen together with all these faces I've never seen in real life. I guess habit is like a stone: once it starts rolling down a particular slope, it just keeps on going. Once I'd gotten used to these online lessons, I then started to feel awkward about meeting people in the flesh. When all your conversations occur through a screen, language starts to lose its color, to grow bland. I was taken by the feeling that, as challenging as it might be, I really wanted to meet with someone in person, and remember the vitality of language. I had the good fortune of getting to know someone who previously taught German at school, and I meet with her twice a week to practice German conversation. She's a real bookworm, so sometimes we use novels instead of textbooks to study from, and we've attempted some German translations of old Japanese stories. Only when I have the names of Japanese authors in front of me do I feel emboldened to wield my German with confidence.

I've been hearing strange rumors—I imagine you've heard them too—about the Pluto post. That the model of Pluto, having been removed from the Planetenweg, which you showed me, has been sighted in its original position again. There have been excited groups of people coming by the Max Franck Institute. Occasionally they split into two groups, to try to ascertain whether the post exists in two places at the same time. The Institute is close to where I live, so I can spot them immediately. Maybe some of their fervor has rubbed off on me—I've occasionally stopped by the Institute myself while out shopping or walking, to check on it. The Pluto post erected after it was removed from the Planetenweg remains in its new location, so maybe it's the ghost of the Pluto post that's appearing by the Bismarck Tower. I'd like to visit sometime and see for myself.

Pluto may have been cast out from the list of planets in the solar system and redesignated as a dwarf, but there's no change to its orbit, right? The Planetenweg now ends with Neptune, and yet that's merely a change brought about by an expansion of our understanding—of course it doesn't mean that the Pluto lying beyond that has actually vanished. It's not a change that shakes the very foundations of our understanding of the universe, like the shift from the geocentric to the heliocentric system, for example. I feel a certain kind of discomfort with the way that kind of line has been drawn. By removing Pluto's classification as a planet, there's a sense that we've automatically forgotten about it.

On the subject of discomfort, I find that as I'm walking around the city, I often lose sight of my destination. I've taken the right road, but the place I'm trying to get to has moved or vanished. Quite possibly, it's a case of being in the wrong time, rather than the wrong place. Encountering those unfamiliar scenes and the people walking through them as I do when it happens, I find myself slipping inside the multiple layers of time that the city contains. I refer to those other layers with the old name for the city: 月沈原. But I also catch sight of other people like me who have slipped into a different layer of time, which reassures me that I don't need to get too worked up about it. As I wrote before, I saw the truffle dog inside one of those slippages, too. He was digging up the ground, very intently.

Changing the subject somewhat, I met a Japanese man called Mr. Terada at my German teacher's house. He's a physicist, and a very quiet person. It's not that he seems reticent in any way—no, it's more like he wears a quietude that perfectly fits him, like a set of well-worn clothes. When I mentioned the other day all of the research into the solar system that's being done at the Max Franck Institute, he seemed very interested, and we arranged that I would go with him to see it. Of course I have no expertise in the natural sciences, and the only things I know about the planets relate to the myths that appear in paintings and all their associated imagery, so I won't be a very good guide. Mr. Terada isn't really one for rhetoric. He prefers to navigate his way through the world in silence, peppered with the odd, brief exchange. I found that quietness of his more interesting than conversation. I'd like to introduce him to you once, when you have the time.

"I heard Nomiya came?"

The evening of the day I received Nomiya's message, I got an unexpected call from Akiko on Skype. In that conversation too, through some unspoken agreement, we kept our cameras off and spoke with audio only. Akiko was the same age as me, and had started her MA at the same time. While I had dropped out of university for a while, she had gone on straight to her PhD, opting to study in Ghent in Belgium. Her doctoral thesis was now in its final stages. While I'd been zigzagging around, she'd been laying down roots in the place where she now lived.

"I got an email from Sawata about it, so I wanted to get in touch and find out. He said you went to the station to meet him, but what happened after that? Are you seeing him often?"

"I actually haven't seen him at all since that first time."

"That figures," Akiko said, calmly. Her way of going straight to the heart of things conversationally, without any preamble, was as it had always been. Back in April, when my plans to visit her had fallen through because the borders had been closed in response to increased infection rates, her distant voice had taken in the situation peaceably.

Akiko's research was on the sanctity of reliquaries in fifteenth century Netherlands. A reliquary was the name for container of holy relics: the remains and the possessions of Christ, the Virgin Mary, and the saints. It was not only the holy figures' bodies that were believed to be holy, but anything they had touched too, and this belief was enshrined into the Catholic faith. Reliquaries served as the vessels for these fragments of bone or teeth, hair clippings and scraps of clothing, and even the tools they'd been tortured with. Owing to their contents, the vessels themselves became sacred, which was reflected in their form and decoration. Akiko's research was particularly focused on Hans Memling's *Shrine of St. Ursula*, a gilded reliquary in the shape of a chapel, whose walls were adorned with intricate paintings depicting episodes in St. Ursula's life. Akiko had chosen this research topic after the earthquake and tsunami.

Akiko's family home had been in Kesennuma, a town whose houses had all been swept away on that March day, and which had subsequently been engulfed by flames, so that nothing of it remained. All her family members had escaped unharmed, but practically every trace of the time that she'd spent there had been lost to the flooding and the fires. After evacuating to her grandparents' house in Matsushima, which had been left untouched by the catastrophe, she returned with her family to where their previous home had been, and looked around for their house that had been ravaged by the waves and the flames. Yet they had been unable to locate any evidence of the past there, everything had been so thoroughly jumbled together. Since then, Akiko had been fixated by our ways of seeing and connecting with objects.

How would she act if she were here? I tried to trace the orbit of her actions in my imagination. Yet wasn't even this kind of exercise ultimately just an excuse? I sighed, and then my true feelings came spilling out.

"I don't think it's a question of my wanting to see him or not. It's rather that I have no idea how to do it."

"And you feel more guilty about it when you think about all those people who've wanted to see him this entire time, or are still waiting for him to come back, right? I can make righteous excuses to myself, saying that it's the current circumstances that are preventing me from going to meet him, but it's harder for you to make excuses, being so close. I know it's unfair to think like this, but I'm kind of relieved in a way. Thanks to all these restrictions, I haven't been forced to directly confront my memories."

"In my case the issue isn't a physical distance so much as a felt one. I keep feeling guilty about how much distance I've allowed to come between me and my memories of that place, and that makes it impossible to face him."

"It's so complex, isn't it? I mean, these are such unique circumstances. It's not every day you need to think about the sense of distance you feel toward a ghost. With nine years having passed, you're confronted with the issue of how to pave over that intervening time that he wasn't present for—but it's not like you can simply ask Nomiya how to do that. What do you think he'll do when Obon is over?"

Akiko was having the same kind of thoughts as Sawata. Even when physically removed from a place we'd been tethered to for so long, our sensibilities were still connected to it. When, like now, I switched back to this language I was so familiar with, I could instantaneously clothe myself in its textures, its sensations. And yet, precisely because of how immediate it seemed, I felt a hesitancy toward speaking it. Are you going to contact him? I sensed Akiko's discombobulation at the question that slipped off my tongue. A moment later, however, her voice had regained its composure.

"For the past nine years, I've been collecting things that I feel some connection with to surround myself with. I feel like I've finally managed to create a distance between myself and the things that have vanished. I think that possibly applies to my memories too. I'm wondering if speaking to Nomiya would mean having to confront that sense of loss again."

I just don't know—the words of hers that she didn't articulate rang out limpidly in my ears. The events of nine years ago had generated a great sense of loss in me, but that was different from any actual loss. The difference between Akiko and me lay in the depth of the loss we'd suffered. Several years after the disaster, when we were both still in Sendai, I'd visited the apartment where Akiko had been living alone. She kept it tidy enough, but still it had a peculiar oppressive ambience about it that made the air heavy. Upon further inspection, I realized that it was crammed full of immaculately ordered objects. Realizing that I was starting to feel stifled by the lack of blank space, Akiko had smiled. "The stuff that I've collected here is all I have to supplement my memories," she'd said. It wasn't only things like books, clothes, and tableware which she'd attempted to give their rightful position—the same treatment was afforded also to promotional merchandise from this and that company, and scraps of paper with things scribbled on them. She'd collected all these things in an attempt to reconstruct the traces of the time that had been lost to the fire and the water. I had no way of knowing whether those items arranged intricately like the tiny pieces making up a stained glass window had succeeded in bringing her memories to the surface. But maybe for her, speaking to Nomiya across the nine-year hiatus wasn't about remembering the past, or recalling certain memories. Maybe for her, beholding the traces of that vanished time would have entailed confronting a loss of memory that continued for her to this day.

The rumors about Pluto weren't broadcast publicly, but they spread quietly among the Göttingen residents, so that after a while this place had come to be treated as a site of pilgrimage. On weekends, groups would gather to visit the spot, and it would become dreadfully crowded. The limitations on numbers of people in outdoor gatherings had eased along with the rest of the lockdown restrictions, and visiting the location for the old Pluto post was seen as a good excuse for a change of scenery. Perhaps because people suddenly felt liberated, even some oddity like this—which easily could have otherwise been treated as a strange prank—called forth people's interest. Maybe the model of Pluto that appeared deep in the forest was afforded mystical status in light of how it came and went, which gave it something of an illusory quality. There were even those who, out of their desire to see the former post, attempted to discover the patterns and laws governing its appearance, analyzing everything from environmental conditions—studying the weather and time of day—to the demographics of its previous witnesses.

These developments also deepened the conflict between the pilgrimage groups that had suddenly materialized and the seasoned forest walkers who'd been frequenting this area long before the Pluto phenomenon. The forest walkers asserted that it was important to engage in a dialogue with nature, that they needed to rest their minds and ears in the serene quiet that couldn't be found in the rest of the city, and that they were alert to any changes in the forest. As the Pluto pilgrimages had grown frequent, there were ever more visible traces of those who didn't understand the forest-going etiquette in that wooded area spreading southeast from the Neptune post, as Agatha had pointed out. Crumpled bread wrappers and empty bottles were left littered around, and the plants were flattened and trampled with footprints in a way that indicated people had been veering off the designated paths. The forest walkers' displeasure at this violation of the forest continued to escalate. Their walking had afforded them a safe place, where they were able to keep a safe distance from others; to have that, too, torn away from them was too much to bear. Their indignation grew progressively louder. Soon the walkers themselves began aiming for the former Pluto site to investigate the veracity of the rumors that had caused all this disturbance. This exacerbated the complexity of the situation still further. Those forest walkers who saw the Pluto post and were taken aback by the mystery of the situation developed some understanding for the pilgrims' position, and sought a form of compromise. Those who didn't see it, however, continued to hold their own position even more stubbornly, eventually taking aim at the more moderate members of their own group. Accordingly, a sense of factionalism had grown even amongst the seasoned walkers.

Meanwhile, there was talk of other subtle changes taking place in the city. If the main issue in the forest to the east was spatial in nature, then the focus in the city to the west was temporal. Fragments of the past had started popping up in town. The memories being reenacted were principally those related to buildings and people. Inside the old town and next to the old buildings forming its perimeter, the buildings from the past were harder to spot as they blended in so well; in those parts of the city where most of the buildings had been rebuilt since the war, though, and in places where people regularly congregated, such as the station and the squares, the buildings that had vanished long ago were immediately noticeable. Some buildings would disappear in the blink of an eye, while others hung around for sufficient stretches of time, taking on the air of a mirage. In that sense, the appearance of these past memories was similar to that of the Pluto post.

But even more prevalent than glimpses of buildings were sightings of people from the past. Figures from old photographs or films in sepia or black-and-white would appear and stroll past. These apparitions were not viewed from within the same cultural context as that underlying Japanese Obon traditions, for example—they weren't hailed as the dead returning to their relatives. The people passing through the present-day scenery simply faded and disappeared, like images that had formed on the water's surface. These occurrences didn't provoke wild rumors, or even much discussion. People allowed these castaways from the past to pass quietly and vanish, without being too bothered or needing to identify them. It seemed likely that in a land such as this, with no tradition of welcoming back one's ghosts, the treatment of visiting memories differed. Maybe here, in this place where so many inhabitants had disappeared over the course of two world wars, those anticipating a reunion with their dead had themselves disappeared inside time. Like a multiple-exposure photograph, the city was projecting its memories onto itself. Yet these scraps of memories were also diluted, like an inferior mirage. With its eyes turned on these multiple layers of time, Göttingen was sunk in deep reflection. It seemed very likely that Nomiya's notation for the city—月沈原—indicated the time belonging to one of those layers.

As the white heat blazed ever stronger, the city assumed a strange luster. Plaster and stone walls revealed their sweaty faces, exuding a peculiarly human, fleshy brightness. Adding to this was the faint smell of smoke that wafted thickly around. I would frequently catch a whiff of something burning, as though there were a fire somewhere just out of sight. In reality, however, there wasn't a single blaze during this time, so it appeared like this was another location-specific memory. The smell made the heat even heavier, and I struggled with headaches. As a result, I barely left the house. I sat at my desk in front of my open thesis, which I'd been making little progress on, staring at the section of the view framed by the window. Agatha had also grown taciturn, and didn't raise the subject of the forest again. Whenever the truffle dog unearthed something on a walk, it seemed to take away a little more of her voice. An unwieldy silence filled the house, with only the sound of the truffle dog's claws scraping the floorboards to stir up the stagnant air.

A few days later, Ursula contacted me. She was going to have a dinner party at five thirty the coming Thursday, and asked me along. She was also inviting Agatha and her dog, partly as a token of her appreciation for the forest walk and her help with the dog's excavations. As my eyes scanned the rest of Ursula's message, I found myself stunned. The message said that she was inviting two other guests: two Japanese people named Terada and Nomiya. She said the pair came to her house twice weekly to practice their German conversation. She'd heard that Nomiya was an acquaintance of mine, she wrote, so it was perfect.

Being a university city, Göttingen was relatively cosmopolitan, but it wasn't large. One would always come to hear, through assorted chains of connections, about what was happening with friends and acquaintances, so that it sometimes felt as though not even the flap of a butterfly's wings escaped attention. Yet Ursula's constellation of relationships was too broad reaching and complex to fathom. To have met Nomiya in the short period since he arrived—not to mention in this period when meeting people was so difficult—was surely something that only she could have accomplished. While I was here dragging my feet, putting off confronting my memories, she'd already connected the dots. Accordingly, my hesitation had been swept away by external forces, and when I reread the message, I felt a jolt of recognition to read the name "Terada." Of course, I thought, this was the name that had appeared several times in Nomiya's email. It seemed it would be impossible for me to ever figure out Ursula's constellation of connections. Just then, an additional text message arrived from her. It was going to be a shell-themed dinner, so if I wanted to bring something, could I make it some kind of shell, or shell-shaped item?

At the mention of this word, the pieces of the sea that were locked away behind my eyes began quietly twinkling at the periphery of my vision. These multilayered pieces had bled into one another to create an odd hybrid. It was born not only of what I had observed, but also constructed from others' words and visions. At its heart though, beneath all those various overlapping associations, lay the sea as I had seen it with my own eyes.

My memories of the sea were wrapped in the soft gauze of childhood impressions. The Ninokura beach in Iwanuma and the public pool next to it—these were the very first threads from which my impressions were spun. Every summer, my parents would make the lengthy drive to take me there, along with my sister, who had a weak heart. *Seawater is good for your body, it'll make you strong*—every summer expedition those same words would be repeated, leaving their traces in my ears. Most of the time, we would start by swimming in the pool and then later move to the beach. When we slid beneath the flickering surface of the water, we found the light had produced patterns that sank all the way down to the depths. The salt water in the pool, which was siphoned from the sea, had a different scent and texture to the water in the public pools near my home and my primary school. Inside that small blue tank of sea, everyone became a brightly colored fish for a spell. When I was menaced by visions of the octopuses and dolphins drawn in white on the bottom of the pool grabbing hold of my feet, I would race for the surface. After a while, my body would grow swollen and tired, and I would stretch it out beneath the sun, lounging and observing as time passed by without so much as a footstep. As the afternoon drew on and we left the pool, we would stand on the beach fringed with green pine forests and stare out at the sea. Unlike the demure lucidity of the pool water, the blue of the sea fluttered between light and dark, unstintingly vocal.

The line of the horizon was sucked into the distant sky, and in the bright sun, the disappearing point was too hazy to discern. Searching for that single point like a mirage, I tried to absorb the phrase "across the sea," but those words themselves seemed far away, beyond the reach of sensation. On the drive home in the car, as my tired, overexerted body in the back seat fell into sleep, I would continue to hold on the quiet clarity that those words summoned, picturing a bright, unknown place hidden away beyond that transparent expanse, as I was jostled around by the rhythm of the water that remained steeped in my body, the distant murmur of the tide stuck in my ears. The afterimage of blue lingering on my eyelids flickered blearily.

Eventually, this sea inside me was overlaid by images of numerous paintings, which yielded new impressions. My connotations with the sea came to include those folds of pale green out of which Botticelli's Venus rose; Caspar David Friedrich's desolate icy sea, with the blue-black shape of the wanderer gazing out mutely at it; the sea as rendered by the impressionists, with its musical depiction of the particles of light and color dancing there; Canaletto's sea inextricably bound to his crisp renditions of Venice; and then the peaceful blue gaze of the sea meeting the sky in Albrecht Altdorfer's *The Battle of Alexander at Issus*. This final version merged with the sea as Nomiya had described it. The peaceful times before dawn, or after sunset. The dialogues in blue that one witnessed there. Even as it served as a giant mirror reflecting the sky through which the colors flowed and passed, the powerful force of its current eddied and whirled around beneath.

Yet the impressions making up this stratum had been swallowed up by the sea that March, and had vanished. None of my own memories of water were violent. I was one of those who'd watched those video clips of the sea as it destroyed everything—those scenes of destruction shown repeatedly on TV and online. That weighty gray, white, and black mass surging through the town, growing heavier with the things it acquired along the way, forming new masses, encroaching still further. Watching these videos, my eyes superimposed on them Nomiya's final moments, which they'd never actually seen.

Those scenes of agony that my eyes took in, the spatial and temporal holes gaping wide open in a way that could never be depicted in a painting, covering over all my other connotations. What I saw in those photos and videos hadn't integrated with the impressions of the sea that lived inside me. Now, there wasn't so much as a trace remaining of the pool I'd visited as a child. The pine forest, too, had been irrevocably damaged by the sea's violence. Since seeing the destruction, the places that I'd visited had been ripped apart into tiny fragments, which returned my gaze in inert silence. This was the silence of words that had been stewing for too long. The severed words of the dead, the words of the survivors that now had no place to go—these lay soaking endlessly inside me alongside the voices in my memories.

I was terrified of speaking to Nomiya in words that contained any more than an indirect perspective on the matter. Even here in Göttingen, he didn't speak of that day of severance. I didn't ask about it, either. The reason it was left unsaid wasn't because I was living and he was dead. Rather, it was because of this indirectness of my stance, my sense of distance from the sea and the nuclear power plant. My perspective lay perpetually outside of the frame. From there, all I could do was gaze at that place inside the canvas that had been erased, and at the sea as it returned to how it had always been.

The day of the shell dinner, I left the house before Agatha. In the morning, we had baked madeleines in little shell-shaped baking molds. Shellfish in Germany were expensive, and I didn't often see them on sale, even in the seafood chain in town named Nordsee—the North Sea. On the rare occasions they actually carried fresh scallops, lying softly atop their bed of ice, their price put them out of my reach. So we pulled out the madeleine baking tray buried deep in the kitchen shelves. By early afternoon, the cakes that had swelled into rounded shell shapes were heaped on top of the table, waiting to cool. I ate one with a cup of tea, under the pretext of testing the flavor, but my memories weren't roused in the slightest—they didn't stir from their hazy slumber, didn't yield a single association. Disguised as a fragrant spice, the thorn of irony had slipped in amid the sweet smell of the cakes.

By then Nomiya and I had exchanged a few messages about the shell dinner party. This occasion that Ursula had facilitated served to bridge the gap between us. We still hadn't spoken with video or even over the phone, but I felt relieved to see the way that our words, as messages, were quietly creating some kind of pattern. With recent developments, people had grown accustomed to maintaining a spatial distance between themselves; analogously, it seemed that for the moment, the two of us had decided to defer the issue of the temporal distance between us. The name Terada had cropped up several more times in Nomiya's messages. Each time I read over his words, I couldn't shake off the sense of a temporal rift separating us. This wasn't caused by anything as simple as Nomiya being a ghost—rather, the ghosts seemed to be the scenes of the city summoned in the gaps between his words. Nomiya would often go on walks with Mr. Terada, or he would visit his lodgings. There he met other people studying abroad from Japan: actresses, students, teachers, people in law-related professions, and so on. It seemed that his life was assuming a rhythm. Recently, he and Mr. Terada had been to see *King Lear*. What was this twin sense of deja vu and jamais vu that I felt—like a sepia photograph? I had the unwavering sense that Nomiya's trips around the town had all been torn from someone else's memories.

Returning again and again to my strange correspondence with Nomiya, I left the apartment and wondered in the direction of Saturn. I'd been planning to go straight to Ursula's, but I ended up leaving the house two hours before I was supposed to be there, so I decided to take a detour. Allowing my legs to determine my direction, I passed through the heavy sunlight of the main road and turned into the network of narrow streets leading off from it like branches. Heading for Theaterstrasse, next to Saturn, I passed alongside Albaniplatz, which was drenched in sun, when my nose detected a smoldering aroma, as though the sun was charring the ground. This was the origin of the smokiness that lingered persistently around this part of town. In May 1933, the Nazis had ordered a book burning to take place in this square. A small plaque had been set into a stone wall to commemorate the occasion. The Heinrich Heine quote inscribed there—"Where they burn books, they will ultimately burn people too"—stood heavy, black, and silent, its expression uncorrupted by the sun.

By now, as I was walking around the town, my eyes had grown accustomed to perceiving palimpsests of time. It was the scars of war, in particular, that drew my attention. As a key transportation hub connecting Germany's main cities, Göttingen had been bombed eight times during the Second World War, with the air raids centered around the railways and the factories around the station. Two of the raids had destroyed the buildings on several streets of the old town, claiming the lives of those inside. Remnants of that time continued to surface today, in the form of the unexploded bombs that were still occasionally discovered. In 2010, an unexploded bomb in Schützenplatz to the northwest of the station had detonated as it was being removed, killing three workers. Ursula and Barbara, who lived in the old town, described how one June night after the long day had come to a close, they heard something like the sound of an explosion: a violent blast that struck the light gray sky, and the clamor of sirens that followed. The cold, unsettled voices of the past still appeared from deep in the earth, like fungi.

As in other places, the city also carried the memories of the numerous people whose lives had been driven out. The attacks on the synagogues, the deportation of Jews to the camps. Memorial plaques and statues made the voices of such people visible—and thus, too, that time, those memories. The city wasn't large, but it contained many such commemorative monuments. That bygone period lurking in this place cast an intense shadow. The hope was, in making those memories visible and joining them together, to give shape to the voices of the dead.

As I looked at the city, the place I'd once lived would quietly flicker past, a pale shadow. There, memories of the sea's violence assumed particular shapes: monuments attesting to the dangers of tsunamis, the remains of a school where many people had lost their lives. How should we carry with us the memories of those who had disappeared to the other side of time? Was it a case of endlessly tracing their contours in our memories, until their names were eventually rubbed away, forgotten? The sea, which contained so many like Nomiya who'd never returned, didn't bear their names—it was always people's memories that did so. Nine years later, they continued searching, quietly yet unceasingly, to bring home the dead who had vanished into the sea.

Even knowing that the city of Göttingen contained dark, bitter elements to its memories, like the rings of a tree, I was still enticed by the impression it left on me—the twisting alleys and dead ends that my feet traced, the lush greenery spilling forth, the movement of all kinds of shadow patterns woven by the sun. Wandering around someplace, without any particular focal point, letting my eyes roam across the scenery in front of me, I would find a portrait of the city, of that particular location rising up before me. When I saw a new face of this kind that I couldn't comprehend except through my feet, my eyes would do their best to understand how it had shifted over time. The multiple faces buried within the strata comprising numerous eras and memories would merge, then peel apart. The city reflected those different faces in flashes, like the blinking of an eye—including the face from that time when it had been known by those three characters, 月沈原.

Tracing the portraits from various times with my eyes, my feet kept on pushing forward, until I reached a white plastered building with a red wooden frame creating a geometric pattern. This was the Junkernschänke—squires' tavern—which dated back to the fifteenth century. The building had changed expression through the decades depending on its owner: from private accommodation to a vacant house, from a hardware business to a wine dealership. Its traditional wooden structure had sustained considerable damage in the March 1945 air raid, but over time, repairs had restored it to its original form. The walls were decorated with pictures rendered in multicolored wood, a number of faces peering out from small circular portraits. The sets of eyes peering from those portholes onto a distant time belonged to seven astrological gods: those for the planets from Mercury through to Saturn—excluding Earth—plus those of the Sun and the Moon. Coincidentally enough, the seven planets as they were classified at the time of the geocentric system were preserved here, right inside the old town. The swords, scepters, bows, and other objects that the gods bore so carefully were drawn according to traditional symbolism. Here, too, their attributes protected them from anonymity, bringing their names into relief.

My promise to be at Ursula's at five thirty still stuck in the back of my mind, I found myself drifting mindlessly through the old town. When I finally snapped back to myself, I realized I was close to the Jupiter post. My trajectory had halted right in front of the decorated window of the oldest confectionery shop in town, and I was staring in, captivated by the Baumkuchen's narrow loops. With its intricate concentric circles, it seemed to be representing not only the rings of a tree as its name suggested, but also the movements of the stars and orbits of the planets. There were several of the ring-shaped cakes stacked on top of one another, not revolving but standing still in the decorative window, caressed by the gazes of people walking past on the other side of the glass. I tore my eyes from the model of the planetary orbit in cake form and headed to Ursula's apartment.

The apartment door opened, and after a very brisk greeting, Ursula returned to the kitchen. In the living room, a man was sitting alone in a chair by the window. Putting down the teacup that had concealed his mouth, he turned toward me and nodded in silent greeting. On the table sat a partially eaten Jupitertorte and, in front of an empty chair, a fork rested on a plate patterned with brown powder and traces of cream cheese. The way the chair had been pulled back intimated the movements of the person who'd gotten up from it. As I was observing this, Nomiya appeared at the door. With a smile on his face, he introduced me to the man by the window, who turned out, as I'd suspected, to be Mr. Terada. To my eyes, Nomiya appeared to have thickened out, and taken on more color than when I saw him at the beginning of July—although maybe it was only because I was seeing him as ghost that invited such comparisons.

The shouts and singsong voices of children came drifting in through the open window. The blinding white of the summer days had delayed their return home. I was fairly sure that Agnes wasn't among that group of voices—most likely, she was inside with Barbara, where the world felt more straightforward to her. At that moment, Agatha and the truffle dog arrived. When she and Nomiya greeted one another, he asked the dog's name: "I've heard about the truffles, but we somehow didn't get around to the subject of his name." Agatha laughed, and informed Nomiya that his real name was Hector. His eyes smiling, Mr. Terada petted the truffle dog's head. Ursula entered the room, and the gathering grew palpably effervescent. As this was going on, the table was being set with plates, glasses, and the breadbasket, and we eventually sat down around it, not according to any seating arrangement.

Ursula had cooked a large amount of moules marinière. We dipped the toasted baguette in the white wine sauce, fragrant with the scent of mussels. Ursula had prepared sour cream, finely diced scallions, and parsley for us to add in case we got bored with the taste of the broth. The taste and smell of the sea, my first in such a long time, radiated out from my mouth through my throat, its colors opening up like a flower.

"They're so delicious I feel as though Botticelli's Venus is about to pop up from one of them," Nomiya said with a straight face, and both Ursula and Agatha laughed.

"What she's standing on in that picture is a scallop shell, and in German the word for scallop is Jakobsmuschel," Ursula explained. "Although it's clams that we call Venusmuschel—Venus shells." With clear fascination, Nomiya nodded, saying, "I guess a clam wouldn't give much stability underfoot."

"What does a clam look like again?" Agatha asked, so Mr.

Terada pulled out a notebook and drew the shape of a shell in careful fountain pen lines, scribbling words to add to his explanation. My tongue loosened by the relaxed atmosphere, I pointed to the shell-shaped pasta in the salad that Nomiya had brought, saying, "They're larger than those, at least."

Nomiya and Mr. Terada seemed to be familiar with Ursula's apartment and this dinner table of hers. Nomiya wore a neatly ironed blue summer shirt, while Mr. Terada had on a starched white shirt with a dark jacket on top, which made me wonder if he wasn't too hot. He had a mustache, and his narrowed eyes seemed to see right through everything around him, quietly and calmly. The distinguished way he comported himself gave him the air of a capacious tree, but his slightly stooping shoulders added to the sense of how petite he was.

After the main course, the madeleines were carried out and set down on the table along with a bottle of white wine Mr. Terada had brought. The wine had a picture of a shell on its label. Ursula wasn't the kind to let the rhythm of an interaction dictate her speech, as a cicada or a bird might do, but she had the special ability to ride whatever current of conversation faced her, always managing to make it to the other side without difficulty. She could sense the sharp rocks lying along the riverbed and the places where the current flowed rapidly, and would casually steer the conversation past these obstacles. When Agatha asked about where Terada and Nomiya were from, and was venturing deeper into the details of the past, Ursula gently redirected her question in a way that made me wonder what she'd already learned. I hadn't explained anything about Nomiya to Ursula or Agatha. Today, while making the madeleines, I'd thought several times about confiding in Agatha about the matter—telling her how Nomiya's thread of time had been severed. However, as I watched the cakes filling out and turning golden brown in the oven, my words and my feelings had shriveled, and I found myself incapable of explaining anything at all.

Now, Ursula asked Agatha about her recent forest walks. To Nomiya and Mr. Terada, who hadn't heard about the truffle dog's excavations, Ursula explained about the objects that it had been finding in the woods by Neptune, instead of the asteroid-shaped fungi. Seeing that the subject had roused their interest, she said: "Would you like to see?"

Sensing us all getting up, the truffle dog opened its eyes and followed us. After finishing his meal, he'd fallen into a full-bellied slumber, apparently unaffected by the proliferation of people. Standing outside the door in the hall across from the bathroom, Ursula reached for the light switch. Even before she'd done so, the truffle dog snuck through the crack in the door, dissolving into its darkness.

The room resembled an exhibition space in a small art museum. The books had disappeared from the shelves lining the walls, and in their place was an arrangement of the objects that the truffle dog had dug up. Even greater than my surprise at this transformation to the study was my amazement at just how many bizarre objects had been accumulated.

With each visit to the forest, the truffle dog had grown increasingly adept at unearthing more odd and out-of-place objects. It was Agatha's role to pick these up and carry them home. Sometimes, Ursula also joined them on these forest walks, or took the truffle dog instead of Agatha. Ursula had taken possession of the objects found on these walks, and was now storing and displaying them in this room. I had the sense that, of all of us, it was Agatha who was most shocked by this development—that she hadn't, previously, understood what Ursula had been doing with all of this stuff. Quite possibly she'd believed that Ursula's interests lay in trying to protect the environment of the forest.

Ursula pointed out the objects displayed on the shelves in the manner of a tour guide, without any particular enthusiasm. A baking tin for bread, an old artificial rose, a few toy arrows, an empty perfume bottle, keys, a wooden cane, a leather-bound book—silently we followed along with our eyes and ears, responding to the movements of her fingers and her voice. On closer inspection, I saw a number of wooden body parts among the ranks of other objects: arms, teeth, feet, nails. Their surfaces were as smooth as resin; despite being severed parts, they'd been fabricated like this, as separate entities.

Even after Ursula's tour had concluded, I still felt unclear about the significance of this room. It felt far too dense with meaning to be simply a storage space for junk. What had once been full bookshelves were now cluttered with objects, indistinct in their purpose, and the now-homeless books formed sullen piles everywhere else—on the floor and strewn across the bedroom, kitchen, and living room. The white walls that the removal of the books had left exposed looked somehow like an unmasked face—a face that belonged to nobody. Trying my best to hide my sense of discomfort while I listened to what Ursula was saying, it finally became clear to me that the aim was not to collect, but to return. Apparently claimants had begun to come forward, declaring themselves. She had already returned some of these items to several Thursdayers.

"Returned them, you say?" Agatha said in surprise. "But it's just trash that Hector found in the forest! Who would want that?"

"When Lucia and Katharina came round, they showed me the photos you'd sent. Someone else who'd happened to be here at the same time also looked, and was struck by an item in one of the pictures. When I first started bringing home the things the truffle dog had dug up, I received a message from this person, saying they hoped to claim that particular item. Then word spread, and before I knew it, I'd become the person responsible for finding objects and returning them to people. Of course, it doesn't work that way with everyone. Some people find an object that resonates with them, but then they refuse to claim it, and others do so only after much deliberation, over the course of several visits. Then there are the people who take things home but end up bringing them back because it was too hard to have them around. It's really up to the person in question to decide. I don't know how long this will continue, but I have no intention of forcing things on people. Although it would be nice if I could clear up enough space to put my books back."

Agatha cast her eyes from shelf to shelf, a look of confusion on her face. Each time her gaze momentarily caught one of the objects, her composure would scatter into pieces, raining down in a shower of fragments. My skin began to twitch ominously with the same discomfort Agatha was now feeling. The fragments lining the room in an unbroken procession didn't adapt themselves to their surroundings—they didn't seem to create a single impression of the room's owner. This accumulation of objects could never come together to form the kind of complete picture that represented the time or the memories of a singular person. Their stifling density transformed itself into a gaze that bore into me. This place resembled Akiko's room, it struck me, and thus the memories lying here were superimposed with the image of another collection.

"Is there anything of yours in here?"

This quiet, impassive question flew out unexpectedly from Mr. Terada's mouth. Up until that point he'd been focusing his scrupulous gaze onto the things on the shelves, maintaining his distance from Agatha and Ursula's interaction. As if reflecting Terada's expression, Ursula's eyes took on a more peaceful hue. She moved toward the door, took down something hanging from the coat hook and held it out for us. It was a cloak in white, gray, and bright lemon-yellow, which fastened at the neck. "This was what tickled my memories." The old cloak swayed with the sound of Ursula's pallid voice.

Thrown off course by our visit to the collection room, the shell dinner party drew to an unsettled close. As we were leaving Ursula's flat, we all tripped over our words, and only Terada managed to say a proper thank you, in a quiet, resonant tone. The four of us decided to do a counterclockwise loop of the city, walking around the wall surrounding the old town. It was half past nine, yet a faint lightness still lingered in the sky, casting vestiges of blue light down upon the town as well. Between the gaps in the trees we caught glimpses of the city. The sun was setting earlier, little by little, and the crispness of the air informed my skin that a change in the seasons was drawing near. White won out over black on the truffle dog's tail, which retained a bright afterglow even in the dimming dusk. With that tail as our beacon, we walked on, gazing through the trees at the house lights that blinked on as we passed by. Mostly, we didn't converse, but simply savored the twilight air. In the place of words, our synchronized footsteps traced the outer rim of the town, which had determined our route. Nomiya asked where along the city wall was the scale model of Saturn. Observing Mr. Terada's puzzled expression, Agatha and Nomiya took turns explaining the Planetenweg. Somehow, this quiet soul who was perpetually listening to others seemed to have missed out, up to this point, on discovering the models of the solar system positioned throughout the city. The topic interested him, though, and he displayed a calm enthusiasm to see the bronze post for Saturn.

While we were talking about the Planetenweg, the truffle dog had apparently found something, and began pressing his nose to the ground, scratching intently at the soil with his front paws. He was getting more and more excited, the movements of his limbs growing progressively faster, until he was using his whole body in his quest to overturn the earth. By now, night had fallen in the forest. The city lights hung far off in the distance, and in their place, the lambent moonlight painted the shadows both fainter and darker. In this nighttime shadow play made up of the different layers of forest, the earth exuded a crisp, cold fragrance. But it wasn't the scent of those black asteroid mushrooms. Rather, it seemed to be a remnant of someone's memory, the breathing of time as it was coming undone. In the dark of night, we stood still and upright, emulating the silhouettes of the trees. Not reacting to the chilly scent that permeated the forest around us as, that buried time coming into contact with the air, we stood in silence, watching the truffle dog digging. A soft white object rose up from the ground. A shell, one of the trees said in surprise. The object that the dog had dug up was a scallop shell.

It was only Agatha who wasn't at all surprised by this, looking on as the truffle dog continued frolicking in the soil. He's dug up a lot of shells recently, she said. Her voice was impassive, dissolving into the night air along with the scent of the earth. At first she'd thought they might be fossils, but he only ever dug up scallop shells. The secrets of the forest that only the dog understood had swelled to proportions too weighty for her to grasp. Watching him, her surprise had transformed into a heavy exhaustion amassing deep inside her.

The truffle dog began digging again, eventually unearthing more scallop shells from within the earth. Glistening in the pale moonlight, the shells glowed faintly from within. Nomiya picked one up in silence, running his finger along its grooves.

"St. James's attribute is a scallop, isn't it?" I nodded. "Come to think of it," he continued quietly, "we used to eat scallops a lot at home. When there was something to celebrate, my mother would buy more fresh seafood than she could prepare on her own, and we'd all sit around and have a party while we ate them. I loved scallops. I'd eat them raw or grilled. I only ever thought about scallops as something we got from the nearby sea. We just threw away the shells, and I didn't attach any meaning to them." Listening to him, it struck me—not for the first time—that there were countless different meanings that could be applied to an object. For Nomiya, those scallop shells might serve as a way marker, leading him to his desired destination. That symbol of St. James might also, in a different context, help Nomiya recall his memories of the sea. The buzz of the fishing port and the lively hues of his life along it. The pungent scent the scallops released as they were grilled. The voices of his family members. The sea. After digging them up, the truffle dog didn't even look at the shells that appeared from the earth, one after another. His role, it seemed, was simply to locate the fragments that had been forgotten. You could do the pilgrimage several times over with these, Nomiya said, laughing at the sheer number of them.

Maybe with the truffle dog's help, I thought, we would be able to find Nomiya's body, which had never been returned from the sea. Maybe, using that nose so attuned to the vestiges of memory, he would succeed in locating the place where Nomiya had been buried. Like the Way of St. James pilgrimage route where the scallop shell served as a permit of passage, I thought, over and over, so Nomiya must've been able to access specific places. Was his visit to Göttingen part of something akin to a pilgrimage? I could hardly ask him to his face whether he would someday return from the sea—or, indeed, whether he planned to go back to Ishinomaki or Sendai for Obon. All these censored words, all these hesitations generated a heavy blankness inside me. I'd never been close enough to Nomiya to be qualify as one of those bereaved by his passing. It was for that reason that I was unable to cry, to empty my insides so that I could then be refilled with memories. Outside of March, I had no problem forgetting about Nomiya. Yet, not having enough memories of him to really process my emotions about what had happened, I was unable to calibrate my feelings or my behavior toward this person who'd appeared after nine years in a way that felt natural to me. I imagined Nomiya must have sensed all of this.

When we came to the intersection in the city wall loop, the bracing clamor of the main road came surging in through our ears and eyes. Noise and color spilled out of this place, and yet it seemed somehow like a deep hole. The dense sense of reality inside the forest was severed at this juncture. We verged off the narrow path that wound its way through the circular forest, with the ring of Saturn that overlapped with the perimeter of the old town and then branched off in three separate directions. Agatha and I took the truffle dog toward Saturn, Terada headed toward Uranus, and Nomiya disappeared into the even more distant darkness surrounding Pluto.

Mr. Terada lived at 18 Planckstrasse. When I'd requested his contact details on our city wall circuit, he'd given me the address of his lodgings. He had no cell phone, and didn't use email either. Nomiya and Agatha didn't seem bothered by his lack of any means of communicating that could have saved time or energy. Internally, however, my temporal perspective had begun warping, and the gaps between that and reality produced twinges akin to a toothache.

Near the road that Mr. Terada was staying on was a small square named after the writer Joseph von Eichendorff, where the Uranus bronze post was positioned. Terada lived within the model Uranus's orbit, and yet he had never seen it. Maybe it's something to do with the time gap, Nomiya remarked casually. It struck me then for the first time that it was possible that Mr. Terada inhabited a period of time even more distant than Nomiya's.

A few days after the shell dinner party, as I was tidying the bookshelves in my room, I finally landed upon the reason why Nomiya may have come to Göttingen: because the city featured within the memories of Torahiko Terada. During his period of studying abroad in Germany, after his research in Berlin, Terada had spent about four months in Göttingen—or rather, in 月沈原—between October 1910 and February 1911. In his letters, sent to his family and friends in Japan, the phrase "in Göttingen from October" had started to appear. To his former teacher Natsume Soseki, he had sent a letter entitled "From Göttingen"—where the name of the city transliterated into the Japanese language in yet another way to how it was now: Gecchingen—which presented a written sketch of the city. There was no trace of excessive ornamentation or inflated illusion. Its style, as it tranquilly recounted the span of time from the Nativity through to the New Year, recalled a black ink drawing with a soft detailed touch and plentiful character.

Was Torahiko Terada's presence here one of the reasons that Nomiya had felt the desire to come to Göttingen? I knew for a fact that Nomiya had read his essays multiple times, and that he'd valued his perspective on things, which veered neither too far into the scientific or the artistic, but treated them at root as one and the same. He savored each of those individual sentences spelled out in pellucid language, attempting to instill them in his own thinking. Nomiya never spoke of what he had found there, but his copy bore the traces of his feelings. After the catastrophe, I'd found a book of his that he'd left in the faculty: the first volume of Torahiko Terada's *Essays*, an Iwanami paperback. The pages of that volume, bent at the spine and creased from being opened so many times, was replete with lines traced under those crystalline phrases, illustrating where Nomiya had gone over and over the words in the effort to imprint them on himself.

About two years later, I also began to read Torahiko Terada's work. His prose made me think of a linked set of gestures: waiting for the surface of a pool of water to grow calm, reaching a hand into it, and scooping up a section of the mirror that had formed on its surface. Every time that perspective of his based upon rigorous observation and analysis or his attempts to engage his expertise in addressing a particular problem would turn to the subject of natural disasters and especially to the study of earthquakes, I would feel my memories from that day stirring and shaking. At the same time, I knew that Terada's persistent focus was on people and their ways of confronting natural disasters. Through the reliable laws of perspective, his voice seemed to pierce its way through time to create a way marker far off in the distance. The book I owned, its mouth gaping as if Nomiya were holding it open, was trying to tell me something. It had taken the form of a ghost mimicking someone's hands.

My body was attempting to remember those colorless voices buried in my memory. Waking up one morning, I discovered teeth growing on my back. The first thing I noticed was the strange rustle that the fabric of my pajamas was making. Feeling an itching sensation, I reached a hand down from my collar to touch the skin on my back with my fingers. My nails struck against something hard. Unlike a scab across a wound, its surface was perfectly smooth as my fingers ran across it. Feeling slightly repulsed by the sensation, I sat up, and again brushed my fingers across its surface, first down from the collar and then up from the hem, before taking my pajamas off and standing in front of a mirror, twisting my neck around to see if I could discover what on earth this thing on my back was. A number of small white specks were stuck to my skin like scales. The scales were tooth shaped. I opened the curtain to try to see better, but the clouded sky only provided enough light to make out their location and little else. There were about five of them on my skin, glinting white like a smile. With my eyes, I traced a line between them—unconsciously, I was trying to read them as a constellation. I felt no pain, but they seemed as if they were firmly attached to my skin, so I decided to get changed and leave them as they were.

After a while, though, I realized that they were snagging on the ends of my hair, which by now had grown quite long. This made it harder to ignore what was happening on my back. Again and again, my hands would creep round and I would stroke the place where the teeth were growing. The teeth bit into my hair, tugging my head back. I would then try to extricate the strands, but sometimes the teeth were so ensnared that I couldn't disentangle it. Things would have been more manageable if I could have thought of the teeth like, say, a line of buttons on clothes, but as it was, that image didn't help me at all. The protuberance was bothering me so much that I thought of going to the hospital, but I fell at the first hurdle of deciding whether to visit a skin specialist or a dentist.

But in the meantime, I chose to confide in Agatha. When I explained the situation, lifting the hem of my clothing to show her my back, Agatha fell into a hole of profound silence. Just when I was thinking that she might scream, she declared in a calm tone, "It's nothing serious. It's not a mouth, it's just teeth. It's a very mild case." There were no lips or mouth cavity, she continued to explain—only the three front teeth and two canines had come through. Teeth alone wouldn't be able to speak for themselves, and they could simply be removed. I was lucky there were no molars, she added. I found myself dumbfounded by this weirdly upbeat attitude of hers. "Why would molars be so bad?"

"If you've got molars, it means you've got a whole mouth, no?"

The logic that she shot right back at me was bizarrely persuasive. We just need to remove them, she murmured, heading quickly to the bathroom and then to the kitchen, before returning with a pair of tweezers, a knife, and a couple of spoons, which she set on the table with a silvery clink. She placed those assorted candidates for forceps between the teeth and my skin in turn, gauging which best fit the size of the crack between the two. In the end, she selected a small dessert spoon. As she inserted it beneath one of the teeth on my back, the cold of the metal burned for a moment then eased. She twisted her wrist a little, using the spoon as a lever. The tooth popped out with surprising brevity, offering not even the slightest resistance. "You can see where it had been digging into the skin, though. See here? Does that hurt?" Agatha went on removing the teeth, placing them one by one on a saucer where they chinked like little pebbles, before holding them out to show me. There was no sign of any wet blood—their roots showed, but the teeth were bone dry, like stones that had come off a necklace. The boundary of the body is quite indistinct, after all. It's not uncommon for things to attach themselves or grow there, Agatha went on. But still, it's good that they weren't attached internally, that they were only superficial. You were really lucky.

When Agatha went off to wash her hands in the bathroom, I stared at the teeth on the saucer. Judging by their size, they seemed to be adult ones, not baby teeth. They were neither yellowing nor chipped in any way—in fact, they looked a lot like tiny art objects. I knew that teeth were used to identify people, but to me, the tiny lumps seemed utterly shrouded in anonymity. My thoughts suddenly took a strange turn, and I found myself wondering if these could be Nomiya's teeth. That would mean that parts of Nomiya's body had taken on a spectral life separate to him. These teeth hadn't come from the sea. Was this how the pain inside me had manifested itself? Even if they retained March as their core, my memories were being eroded with time, in a way that resembled nothing so much as missing teeth. The cavities twinged.

Memory as teeth, teeth as memories ... Before I knew it Agatha was back, also inspecting the teeth on the saucer. Why don't you ask Ursula about them? Her voice lacked intonation. They weren't found in the forest, but maybe she'll have some good advice for you about them as attributes. Maybe, I started to respond, maybe these are supposed to be used as an offering to the dead, but then I realized that these words didn't belong to my German vocabulary. My tongue slipped, and the teeth clattered together. I placed them on a paper napkin strewn with blue flowers and wrapped them up carefully. Were these my attribute? The memories that resurfaced every March, the image of the sea baring its fangs, the words that had lost their contours after I'd kept my mouth shut for so long—had the quest to find a form for these unspoken words led me to these strange white shapes?

*

With the teeth wrapped up in my pocket, I walked the path encircling the old town. I knew that my back didn't carry any scars, that there wasn't any pain, but I felt a sense of distrust toward the skin in that part of my body, as though it had been partitioned off from the rest of my body. I tried to soothe that uneasy, unsettled feeling by walking. Like the dancers standing in the old town's center, I would circulate the band of forest around the town's navel, my body and my memories as my dancing partners. The difference between me and the figures portrayed in *Der Tanz* was that I didn't face my partner, but ran in circles chasing an invisible presence. Here, too, I was interacting with a ghost. My memories, my bodily sensations, too, were dance partners that maintained the correct distance from me. How many times would I have to go round before I would catch up with them? Would they then disappear? The feeling of the teeth brushing my thigh through the fabric of my clothes made my flesh crawl, even after everything that had happened, but my legs didn't stray from the track through the forest.

Around the middle of the second week that I'd started taking these walks, I caught sight of Ursula and Mr. Terada from afar, close to the bronze post for Saturn. They were sitting on a bench, conversing quietly. By "quietly," I mean to refer to the way they were sitting with straight backs looking directly ahead, not supplementing their words with gestures or eye contact. In their total absence of movement, the two appeared to have become trees, steeping in that harmonious time that reigned inside the forest. Ursula today appeared in a kind of time slightly at odds with the present. There was that same sense of distance in her appearance that one found in sepia photos and old landscape paintings. Despite the heat, both Mr. Terada and Ursula were wearing clothes that would have been much more appropriate for the autumn weather. Ursula wore a cape of white and gray with yellow patterning, reminiscent of the winter sky, which was tied at her neck. It was the same we'd seen in her collection room, one of the items unearthed by the truffle dog. With it on, she appeared somehow untouchable, as if she'd moved very far away in time, and this impression left me hesitant to speak to her. Yet she had noticed me, and now looked in my direction. She smiled, creating a pattern of tiny waves around her eyes that made the time and distance contract a little.

"We're on a walk to practice German conversation," she said to me as I drew closer and greeted them. "Today's conversation topic is landscapes that bring back memories. Mr. Terada has been saying some wonderful things about fall, and the moon. How he first discovered the German fall in Göttingen, and how it made him recall the Japanese love for the moon. It shows how memory carves a path through the natural world."

"This city reminds me of my hometown," said Mr. Terada.

Remembering how in his letters he'd written about how this town—which the Japanese at the time had referred to 月沈原, the character for the moon there on full display—was beautiful in fall, I felt a sudden twinge. He had arrived this time during summer, a time of year when he himself had not previously visited before, and found himself walking around an altered, unfamiliar place. He was projecting his memories of home onto this city in front of him, in the same way that I attempted to glimpse Sendai through certain fragments here. I thought about the distance separating ourselves from the seasons and natural landscapes of those far-off homes of ours—about how we went about using the word "nostalgia" in an attempt to shrink the sense of distance we felt.

I sat down beside the bench on a suitably sized rock and listened to the two of them talking. Each time Mr. Terada spoke the name of a plant, he would describe some of his memories about it, as if applying slow strokes of watercolor paint. His vegetal descriptions had a glorious structure to them. The figures of the people taking them in hand, the scenery breathing in the background and the fragments of time all linked up to form stained glass panels depicting his memories.

After half an hour or so, Mr. Terada stood up. A number of postcards in his pocket fell out, scattering the ground like leaves. The postcards showed sepia photographs of the old scenes of the city, where it looked, perhaps unsurprisingly, different from how it did now. As I was picking them up to hand them to him, my eyes were drawn to the word "Japan." Seeing that I had noticed this, Mr. Terada smiled. He'd received the news that his teacher was ill, he told me. "It takes time for news to reach me, so I find out about things only belatedly, after the fact. I simply have to wait for the words to traverse that distance." Tucking the postcards carefully back inside his pocket, he clarified with Ursula the date and time of their next meeting, then said that he had arranged to meet a friend. "Are you playing billiards?" Ursula asked brightly. "I know in the contemporary era it wouldn't be permitted for us to associate indoors like that, but back in our time, it's still permitted," he said with a smile.

"For our next conversation practice session, let's discuss Japanese literature. How about we start from the fifth night of *Ten Nights of Dreams*? I still haven't made it to the end of the ten nights. I want to read the next section, and hear your thoughts."

Nodding in agreement to Ursula's suggestion, Mr. Terada then bowed and made his way down the path through the forest. As he moved, the sense of late fall and impending winter faded away. Looking around, I saw that the hues of summer had returned.

Having bid farewell to that time, Ursula opened her mouth and spoke without looking at me: "You'd be better off if you stopped treating the past like someone else's dream."

At these words, the teeth in my pocket began chattering. I thought, suddenly, of the third dream, where a man is carrying a blind child on his back, who predicts his father's thoughts and actions with a whisper. In his terror, the man considers throwing the boy off and running away from him, but then discovers that the boy is in fact a manifestation of something from his past life. A dream where the past catches up with you, clinging onto you and robbing you of the possibility to escape ... Reeling in her gaze that'd been cast deep inside the gaps between the trees, Ursula turned to look at me. The lines across her face, which formed waves in reflection of her emotions, had grown calm. Had she noticed, at that moment, me thinking about my memories from nine years ago? I took out the paper package from my pocket and showed her the teeth. Reflecting the sun's rays, these memory attributes that had grown from my back shone crisply. Maybe, if I didn't put them into words, the dental scales on my back would form a mouth that could speak for itself. Inspired by that image, my tongue finally loosened. I spoke of Nomiya's ghost. Of my memories of the earthquake that were growing more distant in time. The words I directed at Ursula probed the remains of the pulled teeth of my memory, bringing the shape of my pain into relief. Its true identity was the guilt I felt toward Nomiya—my guilt for being incapable of welcoming him properly. Had I been living the intervening years and months since the catastrophe as a mere bystander, a disinterested observer? This was the question I kept asking myself. I was scared that Nomiya would perceive that distance in me, something white and exposed.

When I'd finished speaking, Ursula responded with a deep silence. She listened, taking in my words without interrupting. After a while, she stood up. "Let's go and see how portraits can give form to memory."

We set out walking in a southward direction down the city wall walking route. The light gray cape hid her body, its cylindrical shape making her look like a doll. She pointed out the garden inside the grounds of St. Albani church, which we were able to glimpse through the trees. In 1942, most of the remaining Jews in the city were assembled here, forced to walk to the station in full view of the public, loaded onto trains, and sent off to the camps. Perhaps the city was tracing that memory on repeat, because footsteps sounded audibly on the street, and the shadows playing across the ground seemed to hint at the figures of people being urged toward their death. This, too, was a memory fragment, a vestige left to a particular place.

Ursula witnessed those memories that were bound to locations, and preserved the memories of that lost pain. She returned the items discovered by the truffle dog to the Thursday visitors. Most people who gravitated to her were those who—like the icons of saints carrying objects that symbolized the agony of being tortured—were unable to let go of their memories that were bound up with pain. That was doubtless the same with places, too. The monuments that this town carried on its shoulders, the memories of the scars left on Japan's northeast coastline ... As I was thinking about the attributes for memories that pertained to specific places, we cut through the gap in the north of the wall into the city.

Close to Jakobskirche on Weender Strasse, Ursula stopped and pointed down at the cobblestones. Eight brass plaques glimmered, gold like a row of dentures, the names of the Jews who'd once lived here winking upon their surfaces. These Stolperstein—literally "stumbling stones"—were gold teeth set into the ground. Looking down at them as she spoke, Ursula told me that Stolperstein were installed in the places where people had been carried off to their death or forced into exile. She listed several streets and the names of buildings whose residents had been erased. In this way, a link was created between the names and the places. If there were no actual portraits remaining of the dead, the place itself became a portrait. Göttingen remembered faces in the form of names. By endowing buildings with the ability to become portraits, they had unearthed the memories too, preserving people's names.

As we were saying our goodbyes outside the church, I asked Ursula about the cloak. "Oh, this?" she said, smiling faintly as she spread open the garment that so amply shrouded her. The lining of the cloak was a map of memories, of faces. As she flipped it over, the faces of the dead rose to its surface. I thought of the Shrine of St. Ursula that Akiko was researching—St. Ursula who protected people by enfolding them in her cloak. As my thoughts swirled around this, Ursula spoke: "The faces of the dead will appear when you connect them up with the memory of a place." Spreading her arms gently, she assumed the form of the saint in the icon. "I hope Nomiya can return to the place that he needs to."

Ursula's soft words grazed my ear like a prayer.

It was from that March onward that I'd begun gazing those portraits known as bird's eye views.

The morning of the day I'd set out for Germany three years ago, I'd flown from Sendai to Narita Airport. Looking down from the plane, the coast inscribed a sharp line in the blue. On the inside of that line spread the brown color wash of the land, with just a smattering of buildings on it. It looked as though someone had stopped midway through creating it—an image drawn from memory, trying, and failing, to recreate what had been there before. That vision now rose up in me.

Unable to wipe away the traces of the violence wreaked by the hands of the sea, I was forced to start off with a wash of color—with the very rudimentary preparations for a sketch. When I tried to layer my memories on top of this sketch, a different face, branded with pain, would blot out everything else. I was still unable to revive the portrait that had vanished on the far side of time ripped asunder.

Sometimes, when portraying a certain place or region of the country, the resulting image ends up as not a landscape, but a portrait. A face surfaces amid the patch of land or the town inside the frame. When the artist perceives the changes over time, when those memories are painted into the picture, then it can become a large-scale portrait of a place. As I moved between different locales, I'd gradually begun to be able to tell the difference between landscapes and portraits of places. Maybe one could see it as a question of different perspectives on time. A landscape required a photographic viewpoint and careful observation of phenomena, recording the dialogue between the viewer and the present state of the place. To see the past in a place, though, to turn one's attention to the memories connected with it, a painter had to listen to the monologue that was a specific place's memories. When these conditions were met, the resulting picture would likely turn out as a portrait.

When someone was confronted by the sight of a place that'd been lost, what their gaze searched for was the face of the land before its destruction—the familiar face on which time had left its mark, where memories had seeped into it. Since that day, everyone visiting that coastline had looked at it with eyes seeking that particular face, their gazes fixed on a bygone past.

I'd formed the habit of opening up pictures online of the coastline and the inland locations where the tsunami had struck, and tracing over them with my eyes. Each time, I would think of them as sketches of a particular Michael Ende story, "Eine Schicksalshieroglyphe" (a hieroglyph of fate). During the Second World War, a young soldier is given leave, and rushes to see his girlfriend. The two lovers, who are in a hotel room as the air-raid sirens are going off, choose to prolong their time together instead of taking shelter in the bunker. A bomb falls on the building, and the two are enveloped in its destruction. The man dies, but his girlfriend survives, her face now heavily scarred. Indeed, her face is divided into black-and-white sections—the half that was covered by her lover's body at the point of the explosion retains the original white of her skin, while the other half is permanently marked with the countless black ash particles that the force of the blast implanted into her skin. This two-sided black-and-white face doesn't disappear even after the war; her memories are forever imprinted on her body.

When I looked at photographs that showed the scene on both sides of the Sendai Tobu Road, which had blocked off the tsunami from reaching further inland and thus marked the dividing line between the damaged and nondamaged regions, I would imagine that two-sided face floating above it. There was the half swallowed up by the sea and the half that the tsunami didn't reach—no amount of time or effort could rejoin those two into a whole again. Even if the buildings and roads were restored to exactly how they used to be, that face cleft in two would lie beneath them. Since that day, I'd only seen one half of that face. The other had no voice for me. The voiceless half included not only the coastal towns and cities, but the nuclear exclusion zone from the power plant blast as well. This duality affected how a place was remembered. How many memories could I have of the half that I hadn't actually experienced? Tracing the indirect gaze found in anonymous reports, photographs, and videos in a superficial manner could only help to create impressions, not memories.

I also thought about the white, unscarred half of the face. That half, too, bore its own wounds. Buildings collapsing, landslides, fissures in the road and the liquefying of the land—those were just a few of the things I'd seen happen in inland locales during that silent March. I felt that by splitting the land in half and seeing it as two faces, the memories of it as a single territory would be forsaken. There'd been the destruction to the coast, and then the land being split into two pieces—the place had been broken apart twice over. Each year when March came around, people would attempt to apply makeup—in the form of words about regeneration and reconstruction—onto that ravaged face. Every time they did so, the face that had been lost would rise up like a ghost. In the attempt to keep hiding this face, they were merely attempting to force a mask upon everything that lay underneath.

Visiting Ursula one Thursday afternoon, I encountered Barbara and Agnes again. The season seemed to have suddenly fallen out of step that day—the sky was dark and cloudy, and the temperature dropped as if fall had arrived. Barbara wore a thin maroon and brown sweater. In contrast to those autumnal shades, Agnes's palette was still firmly that of summer—she wore a white tank top under a bright jade-colored zip-up hoodie. When I entered the room, there was a look of great sadness on Agnes's face, clouded over by distemper. Noticing my presence, she moved wordlessly out of the living room, and then walked through the outer door. In her hand she held a small carved wooden ornament. Barbara sighed. Although her features were similar to Agnes's, they were composed into a different expression, and she flashed a soft smile in my direction. Her demeanor was more subdued, alluding to a line she had drawn between herself and her pain. Seeing these unaccustomed looks of emotion on both mother and daughter gave my own feelings a gray tone. As if to hide her expression, Barbara got to her feet and picked up the photo postcard with a picture of a tower that was lying on the table. With just a tired smile, like the trace of a scent, she left the room without a word.

After another moment, Ursula appeared with a pot of tea. Barbara and Agnes have gone home, I told her. Ursula picked up a cup and poured the tea. The cup she handed me was cascading over with the scent of frozen flowers, wintry in color. The discomforting sense of a deep rift pervaded the room and everything in it, muting their tones. Ursula's familiar apartment was sunken in shadow, its expression a mixture of disinterest and stiltedness. The sky outside the window was daubed in heavy cloud, and there was a strange feeling in the air, as if little pieces of all the different seasons had been cut out and stitched together.

"Are they okay?" I asked, recalling the pained expressions on Barbara's and Agnes's faces.

"They wanted to take one of the truffle dog's discoveries home, but it's proving difficult for them. I thought it would be okay, since it's something that exists in both their memories." Ursula said quietly. Tiredness had inscribed waves onto her face, and each time she opened her mouth these waves trembled, so that she appeared to be crying invisible tears. With a sigh, she said, "I think it was particularly hard for Agnes. She's still young."

"She seems very adult, emotionally speaking?"

"Oh, she's just a child. I don't mean that as an insult. Even if she looks and acts much older than her actual age, it won't do any good for the people around her to forget that fact. Adults have to be careful with her. They need to remember that she can't tolerate pain. Not that pain has anything to do with age, anyway. People think they've gotten used to pain, but they've actually just put a distance between themselves and the memories of it. Memories of pain are always fresh. That goes for people and for places."

I looked at the dishes the pair had been using, still sitting on the table. On the little plates set alongside the cups were slices of the Jupitertorte. Both slices had barely been touched. This unfinished treat seemed to serve as an illustration of the powerful sense of rejection and sadness that the highly strung sweet-toothed girl had felt.

Ursula didn't say anything else. She didn't mention the painful memories that the pair's attribute was connected to. In her silence, through the words she didn't say, I naturally arrived at an understanding. It concerned the reminisces of someone who had died, and symbolized a memory of separation.

After cutting me a large slice of Jupitertorte, Ursula looked at me as she asked, "How's your back?"

"There's no sign of more teeth."

At this, her expression finally softened into a smile.

"That's good to hear. It means you don't need to hurry into a decision about what to do right away. When memories take on a visual form, you need to take your time to think about them. And with teeth, there's no worry about them spoiling."

Ursula stopped speaking, and then, after a pause, she asked about Agatha. I related the details of Agatha's profound silence, and Ursula sighed, bringing over a plate covered with a cloth from the shelf. When she lifted the white cloth, I saw two breasts sitting on the plate. Their gentle, rounded forms were a reddish brown. They looked as though, if you were to place one on your palm, it would cower there like a small animal. The surface where they'd been severed was stuck cleanly to the plate, and they didn't seem as though they could easily be removed. These were Agatha's memory attributes.

Ursula informed me, when I inquired, that the truffle dog had found them in the woods behind Neptune. When they'd first appeared, emerging round and white from the earth, Ursula had thought they were mushrooms. The moment Agatha had seen them, she'd grown terribly upset and attempted to rebury them. Ursula had kept her from doing something so drastic, but from then on, Agatha had stopped visiting Ursula, possibly afraid that the subject would be broached.

Even Ursula, in charge of maintaining the room where all the items were collected, seemed unsure of what to do with the breasts. At first, mindful of preserving their freshness, she'd kept them in the fridge, but they'd lost their moisture and grown a little hard. "Besides, with the breasts in the fridge, there was no longer any room for the Jupitertorte," Ursula pronounced, earnestly. At that exact moment, I'd broken off a small section of the Jupitertorte with my fork and put it in my mouth. The cake was extremely soft, transforming inside my mouth to a thick, gelatinous paste. "Tell Agatha. She can take her time, and she doesn't need to take them home, but she should at least see them." Even as Ursula finished these words, the cake was still there in my mouth, forming a lump that I couldn't swallow.

When I got home, I heard a dull clunk of something at my feet as I opened the door to the apartment. I looked down to see an object on the floor that looked a lot like a set of pliers. When I reached down to pick it up, I found it cold and heavy, shining dully in my hands. The object revealed its forbidding form in the soft, early dusk light filtering in behind me: it was a pair of dental forceps, an instrument for extracting teeth, which I had only ever seen before in paintings. I felt my skin twinge in pain as it remembered the teeth that had grown there, but I could hardly drop the implement back down on the floor, so I made my way down the hall with it in hand.

Agatha was sunk deep down into the chair in the living room, looking as though she were glued to its back. When I said hello, she finally turned to glance in my direction. The quiet look in her eyes seemed borrowed from a female saint, eyes turned heavenwards in the depth of her grief. Those eyes transparent as raindrops were full of palpable sorrow. The focus of her gaze settled on the object in my hands.

"What're these?" I said, waving the forceps slightly.

"Hector brought them back from the forest," she said, disinterestedly. It seemed as though she no longer paid any attention to what the dog brought home. Recently, I would find attributes lying around the house. Until now, Agatha had shown resistance to bringing the truffle dog's findings into the house, and had checked the place assiduously for things he might have snuck inside. Yet she seemed to have grown indifferent, now permitting the incursion of these things into the property. The truffle dog himself was forming a puddle-like shape on the floor, dissolving into sleep without a care in the world.

I passed on Ursula's message to Agatha. "She says to come and see your attribute, quickly."

Agatha inhaled sharply, then gave a low laugh, like an owl living deep in the forest. I found myself unable to move. There, hidden behind her laughter, was the sound of a child sobbing—a child on some far-off night, unable to sleep, afraid of the dark and the invisible monsters of the imagination. Agatha had been taken prisoner by the other emotion that lay behind her laughter. With that dual-layered laugh, she was lamenting something.

"They're my mother's," she said, during a pause in her bi-partite laugh. "They're my dead mother's memories." The laughter stopped, just the sound of her breathing punctured the silence.

"You mean those breasts aren't your own memory attribute?"

"Well, they're my mother's, so they're also mine," Agatha responded, with evident tension. "The truth is, it wasn't breast cancer that killed my mother. She took her own life."

In that room filled by the dark shadows of dusk, our shapes and those of the truffle dog were indistinct. Only our voices retained their contours. Her voice directed not at me but at the fading canine form in front of her, she began to tell her story.

Her parents had divorced when she was ten, and Agatha had begun living with her mother and her elder sister. Her mother had worked as a doctor, so they'd had enough money, and quickly adjusted to their new life. Occasionally a new boyfriend of their mother's would be added into their lives, but they all disappeared soon enough, and didn't cause any lasting distance between the women. Eventually, both Agatha and her sister left home to attend university. Thanks to frequent phone calls, the trio remained close in spite of their physical separation.

Three years ago, her mother's breast cancer had been discovered, and it was determined that she would have a mastectomy. The recovery went well, the cancer didn't seem to have spread, and all three were relieved. Half a year later, Agatha got a call from her sister. Her sister had gone to visit her mother, who wasn't feeling well, and her mother had revealed that there were signs the cancer was spreading into other parts of her body. Agatha felt pained and confused, as if she'd been slapped in the face. Her mother didn't live far away, and she'd been visiting her even more frequently than usual. A few days before her sister's phone call, the two of them had been for a walk in the woods with the truffle dog, talking about mushrooms. Yet her mother hadn't mentioned anything about the cancer.

After the phone call, Agatha canceled her plans for her three-week holiday and went to see her mother instead. When her mother greeted her she seemed slightly gaunt, but composed, and welcomed the news of Agatha's long stay. Agatha broached the heavy topic, and her mother began explaining to her in detail the next courses of treatment, and options for hospices. She'd always been a careful planner and, true to form, it seemed as though she'd already decided everything, through talks with Agatha's elder sister. It seemed the only thing that remained for Agatha to do was to ensure as best she could that her own time coincided with that path of her mother's. And yet, at dawn on the sixth day of her stay, Agatha woke to hear the truffle dog's frightened howling, and found her mother had hung herself in the bedroom.

"My sister came right away, and the two of us dealt with everything, as confused as we were. But when things had settled a little, I realized that a distance had opened up between the two of us. There was only one time that she openly confronted me, asking me why hadn't I noticed anything. My sister was closer to my mother than I was, so maybe she felt a deeper pain. But I didn't understand, either, why my mother had chosen to die when I was there. From that point on, we more or less stopped contacting each other. It's only recently that I finally visited her. But it's no good. The shadow of my mother's death still lingers between us."

Several hundred times already, Agatha had gone back over her mother's words during her stay, her state and her mood, trying to find some kind of premonition of what would eventually happen. The way that short period of time leading up to her mother's suicide had been dragged, kicking and screaming, from her memory to have all its details subjected to a relentless examination meant it had taken on a bizarrely narrative quality. In her memory, her mother had given countless indications of what was to come within the flow of her actions, as naturally as if handing her cups of tea. As her memory footage drew closer to the final scene, those signs took on an unbearable obviousness. As Agatha continued to chastise herself for her lack of sensitivity, her memories gradually broke asunder. By the time she'd realized what was happening, the memory of her final moments spent with her mother had transformed themselves. That period of time had become so thoroughly painted over in pain and guilt that it was no longer able to retain its original form. In that sense, Agatha was experiencing memory loss. When she'd returned from Cologne, those scraps of distorted memories had settled in the apartment like ghosts, forever trying to catch her attention. The truffle dog had unearthed the breasts as if capturing a fleeing enemy. Those lost memories clung to her white face uninscribed by any markings, closing off what lay within.

Agatha went to her room and the truffle dog followed after her, both his movements and the noise of his paws like black water. Hearing the sound of her door close shut, I also retreated to my room. The scene outside the window was swallowed up in shadow, and the call of an unfamiliar bird pierced the sinking darkness. Was that, too, a lament? As my eyes and ears projected the scraps of pain they had taken in back onto the scene in front of me, the bird's cry appeared to deepen the night beyond.

On my desk by the window lay a small dish with the five teeth in it. When I switched on the overhead light, the teeth were shrouded in a hazy light, so they appeared to be winking. Like Agatha, I too had been rendered immobile by memories.

I turned on my computer to find Skype messages from both Sawata and Akiko. *I spoke to Nomiya*, and, *I got in touch with Nomiya. We had a long talk*. Brief reports—that was all. Neither told me what they'd spoken about. That wasn't information for me. The memories that were steeping inside them, the nine years of separation, the shape of such things differed from person to person, and there was nothing to do but keep them on your person, these attributes, visible or not; nothing to do but to keep on thinking of that lost place, the place with everything stripped away from it, with a face like that of the people who'd had all of their memories ripped away from their roots. The place where the time that had been frozen coexisted in layers with the time that had begun after the destruction. I still didn't know how near those layered times and places could mix with one another.

Just then, a text came from Barbara, sent out to a group chat. *Would you like to go on a walk to Bismarck Tower on Sunday? Agnes said she'll come. Let's see whether the Pluto bronze post is there or not*. Barbara went onto explain that, after seeing Agnes so out of spirits, she had suggested an excursion. At first Agnes complained that it was too far and she didn't have the energy, but the allure of visiting Pluto with all the others had won out over her doubts, and she'd grown increasingly enthusiastic about the idea. Positive replies from Ursula, Katharina, Lucia, and Nomiya popped up one after another in bubbles on the screen. *Nomiya, please tell Mr. Terada about it*. At that moment, Agatha's reply also appeared, with the words, *I'll bring Hector along*. With this message, I understood that Agatha had decided to confront her own painful memories. I drafted a short message stating that I would go as well, and sent it.

Plato's orbit was elliptical, and for a certain distance, fell within that of Neptune. During that time, Pluto became the eighth satellite in line from the sun. Even without the title of "planet," this fact remained unchanged. Then it shifted from inside to out, going back once again to being the ninth orbiting body. Similarly, Nomiya would likely move on after a while. The time had come for me to speak to him, as Sawata and Akiko had done. The scenery on the other side of the windowpane was drained of color. Reflecting the light from the room, the glass became a mirror; I searched for the vanishing point inside my own eyes. The same birdcall again. Beyond the window, the night was lamenting something.

That Saturday midway through August, the sun appeared bright white in the early morning sky, and the day surfaced as if from a long dream, not disrupting the heavy, stagnant air. Agatha appeared similarly placid. She started preparing for our planetary tour with a look of composure, packing breakfast, two bottles of water, food for the truffle dog, and snacks into her bag. Our bags bulged soft and heavy, as if signaling our expectations for the expedition. Before heading out, I slipped the teeth into the pocket of my hoodie.

On the way to the Sun post, which was our designated meeting point, I noticed that Göttingen seemed somehow different than usual. Each time my feet struck the cobbles beneath, a patchwork of different expressions would rise up and then vanish. They dissolved into nothingness, not leaving any trace of themselves behind, like dreams from an afternoon nap. The expressions that passed across the face of the city were not fixed, but slid between the foreground and the background, appeared and disappeared as they passed through the holes in the lattice of time as through an openwork panel. With each coming step, I moved back in time or lurched forward, and soon I grew so dizzy that my vision began to distort and tremble. The city, it seemed, had chosen today to take a voyage through its memories. Using the assorted ways in which it had been photographed across the years like masks from a summer festival, it was cycling through an array of different looks. I caught glimpses of images I thought to be representing Göttingen as 月沈原, but they dissolved before taking hold in my vision, like a familiar silhouette glimpsed from behind in a crowd.

Beneath a summer sky that shimmered like a candle flame, five shadows were standing beside the model of the Sun. Everyone had arrived except for Barbara and Agnes. Ursula and Lucia stood in the shade of the hotel building to avoid the sun, but Katharina, Nomiya, and Mr. Terada were inspecting the words written on the post, which cast dark shadows on the ground. I slipped away from the group, looking toward the station through a gap in the city wall walking route, and was greeted by a surprise. The cars in front of the station had vanished. Greenery filled the open white-cobbled square, so it looked much like a cool, peaceful garden. Blinking several times, I saw that the scene had another layer underneath, like pencil markings from a draft that still showed through on the paper, and this one was full of sparkling metal.

"The station is ... transforming."

Hearing my voice cracking with surprise, Ursula nodded, unfazed, as if it were the most natural thing in the world. "Yes, it's a memory from before the war."

"It's from around 1910," Mr. Terada asserted quietly. When standing in front of the station, his slender body, which didn't seem affected by the heavy heat, grew perfectly clear in its contours.

"Is this how you remember it?" Nomiya asked with interest, and Mr. Terada smiled silently.

"This area changed a lot since the bombings. It looks so cool and beautiful like this." Hearing Ursula's admiring voice, my nauseated senses regained their equilibrium, and I finally accepted Göttingen's patchwork reminiscences. Barbara and Agnes arrived, and the sound of Lucia's voice pulled our gaze back to the other side of the street. For once, it was Agnes who approached us, her pace slow. It was so hot today that the woods and the tower would probably be half asleep, she said. It would be easy for Pluto to be drawn into that sleepiness too. Hearing these words in her singsong voice, not dissimilar to birdsong, we understood that the cloud that had been floating over Agnes had finally lifted, and our expressions softened.

The number of planets depended on the mood of the city at that particular time—or maybe, the mood of its memories. You wouldn't know whether there were eight or nine planets until you got there. From where we stood by the Sun we could see, across a narrow road, Mercury through to Mars spread out in a line, as if modeling to the city's inhabitants how to maintain the correct social distance from one another. With their bronze feet rooted firmly in the ground, these planetary posts displayed a confident sense of their own time and place. The model orb of the Sun absorbed the heat of the white ball of light in the sky, its hazy contours shining in dull gold. We flocked around it, and from there we began our pilgrimage along the path of the planets to the end of the solar system.

As we observed it, the city was bathed in a gold hue, as if the surface of the model sun had dissolved, overflowed, and coated everything around. We soon reached Mercury; the small planet encased in glass appeared to have parched and shriveled in the heat. Everyone except Mr. Terada was complaining of the sun's heaviness, but still continued walking, afraid that they themselves might wither and shrink too.

Clouds had appeared, and for just a moment, the sky turned dark and heavy. Even when the sun was obscured by clouds, the dense heat remained trapped in the air, with nowhere to go. With the sense of the clouds' mass rendering us speech-less, we passed by Venus. By the time we came to Earth, the clouds had disappeared and the sky was a bright blue. Darting a birdlike glance at the post, Agnes screeched in surprise. Earth was broken. When we all peered in hastily, we saw that the glass containing the piece of bronze representing our planet was cracked, as if torn in two. This disturbing phenomenon provoked a burst of animated conversation. As I looked at the crack, I thought once again to the earthquake of nine years ago. The energy released by that huge earthquake in March had skewed the axis of the earth; the shock had been released as waves that traveled into space beyond Earth's atmosphere.

When we neared Mars, a fleet of passing cars sent red dust flying into the air. We waited for it to settle until we could see where we were going, then continued down Goethestrasse. Moving forward carefully, making sure we didn't stir up the red dust again, we refrained from speaking so the particles suspended in the air wouldn't get inside our mouths. Our movement was as slow and careful as that of a probe vehicle. The blue of the sky was paler and less clear, as though it too had been shaken with dust. Beneath the bridge, where the name of the road changed, ran the slender river that snaked through the city. Looking down, I noticed some lantern-like objects with small candles inside floating along the river with the seagulls. There were lots of them, forming a line. Though the candles swayed from side to side with the gentle movement of the water, their flames remained lit. Each an al-legory for a person's lifetime, they were gliding along through another, capacious expanse of time.

Approaching the place where the road intersected with the main street of the old town, we saw Jupiter. Beyond it, the fro-zen momentum of the dancers leapt vividly into my eyes, even at this distance. The buildings on either side that I'd always believed to be old were now flitting back and forth through memories, ruining my temporal perspective. The sight of them suddenly wearing the face of another time seemed deliberately designed to tease. We were passing through the portrait of a city that had worn so many different faces, looking at it while remaining unsure if we were appreciating it as a work of art, or witnessing its history. The trio of dancers whirled around energetically, their bodies moving with the fluidity of water and their spinning bronze musculature shining in the sun. The numerous masks that were ripped from their two faces became photographs and postcards in the air—words directed at someone now far away. Images flashed before my eyes: three laughing children, their dark eyes opened wide; a teenage boy in a straw hat grinning; a family portrait with all its members beautifully attired in their best clothes, standing frozen to the spot. The faces of the ones who'd been erased. The fragments of time lingering there in the photograph conveyed that they had been here, that the place carried their memory, and that there were people to observe and hear those memories.

Looking further into the distance, I saw a number of small festival floats making their way closer to us from the direction of Saturn. Pulled along by invisible hands, the floats turned near to *Der Tanz*, making their way toward the square outside the former city hall. The parade seemed to resemble the academic procession through Göttingen held in celebration of the graduation of the doctoral students, featuring large hand-pulled carts decorated with paper decorations and balloons. After the graduation ceremony at the university, the doctoral graduates would be crammed into the cart along with boxes of beer and champagne and bouquets of flowers, and the carts would be pushed as far as the *Gänseliesel* statue in the square, while people played music and sung loudly. According to local tradition, the doctoral graduates would kiss the cheek of the bronze statue showing the maiden holding her geese, decorating it with bouquets of flowers.

Yet this procession carried with it only silence. There were no musicians or singers in sight. When I strained my eyes, I could make out the traces of fifteenth or sixteenth century paintings dotted here and there. The seven evenly spaced floats progressed in a line. A woman stood holding a burning heart and arrow in hand, her long hair and the light robe covering her body fluttering in the wind. A man in an imposing suit of armor held up his sword perfectly upright like a scepter. Everyone, even the musician raising his instrument to his mouth, even the hunter with his bow and arrow, all held up their attributes in the glittering sun, tearing off the mask of anonymity that the distant past afforded and exposing their faces. The afterimage left in my eyes each time one of the floats passed seemed to merge with the seven planetary gods rendered on the wall of the Junkerschänke. On the sides of that building restored after its destruction during the air raids, the astronomical gods from the geocentric age revealed their faces—faces that were the same, and yet different. The more layers of time atop one another, the more mixed the imagery grew. Working to override the impression of the historical prints were the fluttering paper decorations, which spilled over from the floats and hung down their sides. Each time they swayed, they would conceal the figures inside, creating a flickering effect that made it hard to comprehend who was sitting there. The hubbub of the main road also receded, and the procession made its way amid the silence of water. The leaflike rustle of the paper decorations created a sound like a flock of birds all flapping their wings at once. Long streamers fluttered from decorative paper balls, tracing the currents of the wind and the water in the air. Each float was decorated in a different color, in all assorted shades of light and dark. The sound of the rustling paper, which reflected sonically that rolling gradation in hue, filtered in through my ears, stirring up my memories of color, of other places. It's Tanabata, I heard Nomiya murmur between intervals in the cacophony of the paper.

This procession of the planetary gods brought up memories of the festivals in Sendai, where both Nomiya and I had been. Around the time of the Tanabata festival, from July through to early August, the station, the road in front of it, and the various shotengai in the city would be strung up with paper decorations. The sensation of the streamers that flowed down like cascading waterfalls touching my face, the gentle rustle of that taut paper, and the shadows of the passing colors had all reminded me of water. By the time the festival neared its apex, the flow of people passing also assumed the weight of an eddying current, and I kept my distance. Yet in the early morning or late at night, when even the rustling of paper ceased, you could observe that colored water flowing from one end of the arcade to the other, trailing off into the distance. The assorted floats of the planetary gods that now went past emulated that quiet coloration, coinciding with Nomiya's appearance of recalling a distant reality, before they and the murmur of paper disappeared entirely.

We continued walking, like pilgrims of time, pilgrims of memory, though we carried no shells to vouch for our identity as such. All one needed to pass down the Planetenweg was one's own memories, our memory attributes. Ursula carried pieces of the memories belonging to the city, and to other people. She listened to the words of others, silently carrying the memory scraps she'd received, digging up the memories of those who'd disappeared in the war, emerging from her silence to pass these onto someone else—over and over, she repeated this cycle. The memories of people and places sewn in layers on the inside of her cloak were connected to the Thursdayers and their own memories and sorrows, forming complex constellations. Inside all those intricately overlapping layers of time, her quiet, steady footsteps, which never erred from the path ahead of her, rang out. Agatha's steps were tracing the outline of her mother, who'd taken her own life, and her final few days. From within that place where her memories had already been transformed, she extended a painful gaze, attempting to once again reconfigure her mother and her mother's death. The truffle dog, who'd been her mother's calm companion through that time, stayed close beside her, gently licking her hand. Mr. Terada, who'd walked through Göttingen when it was 月沈原, traversed a wide, silent path of memories. His lucid perspective turned toward the natural sciences and literature. The crystallized form of all he had achieved with his own hands in physics. The knowledge he had bestowed on the societies of the future, through his own experience and observation of natural disasters. His memories of Göttingen, which were squeezed in between all those other aspects of his life. Even so far away from the place and time that his home, the distance was compressed by his words. Lured by those very words, Nomiya had arrived here from across that temporal rift. The families and the places erased by the disaster of nine years before, all the vacant time that had elapsed while he still hadn't returned home, the memories of far-off Sawata and Akiko, the memories tied to the layers of time that existed in this city, the heft of the time Nomiya had spent—all of these had become the feet that were now treading this strange ground. The memories of the disaster that had torn people's bodies apart and all of the time that had passed since then had made a pilgrim of me, setting out for Pluto. Even if the memories leading a sloped line back to nine years previously had come to me in the form of teeth, I still needed to make my own way down this planetary route to see with my own eyes where it actually led. This time I would remember the orbit that Nomiya had traced.

The further I walked, the more memory fragments rose up before me. Pieced together, they resembled panes of stained glass—perhaps they even formed icons, or scenes from the lives of saints. The feet treading the Planetenweg interlocked beautifully with the rhythm of my memories. Katharina, Lucia, Barbara, and Agnes were also walking through the time that their memory attributes evoked. Ursula's collection room, the photographs Agatha had taken, and the truffle dog's discoveries—the memories that had risen up from these accompanied us on our journey, connecting the spaces between the planets.

As we moved from Jupiter to Saturn, looking up at the sky where swirling clouds formed a pattern like that of maroon roses, we encountered lots of photographic memories of the city. A woman with a long skirt, gloves, and parasol turned the corner. An elderly woman wrapped up tightly in dark clothing appeared from the door of a bakery. A girl in a white summer dress and a boy in a sailor suit went running down the street, and some people who looked Japanese walked past. Wearing suits and carrying walking sticks, the Japanese men glanced at Mr. Terada and raised their hands to him in greeting. "They're fellow international students." Having raised a hand in greeting, Mr. Terada watched the men walking off, chatting and laughing with one another. Young men in stiff uniforms strode imperiously down the street, with the targets of their pursuit in sight. We walked through the town's memories, slipping by those recollections that originated from the realm of black-and-white photographs. People's memories would swirl around us in multiple layers, and as our eyes traced them, the rhythm of our feet ran the risk of being thrown off kilter. Past this riot of memories, we finally arrived at Saturn.

With Saturn behind us, we came to the residential area of

the city—we were no longer in the old town. The city continued its reminiscing, but we'd been freed from the intensity of its bustle, our ears regaining the tranquility of quiet. We passed by Theaterplatz, where the theater still was, and then headed east along Planckstrasse. Strolling amid the dreams of time, we threaded our way past places and people we'd seen in photographs and films. We walked by number 18 where Mr. Terada stayed, then, five minutes later, we reached Eichendorffplatz. Moving up to the Uranus bronze post, Mr. Terada turned his gaze on the small model planet encased there. Uranus was shown as a small orb perched atop a mound, so it looked a little like the morning sun rising up from behind a mountain. Seeing that oddly Japanese image, I realized that this was the first time Mr. Terada was seeing the Uranus post. Spatially, he was very close to it, but temporally, very far removed. The wind rustled through the trees, its sound carrying with it the familiar feeling of fall, which concealed the signs of summer. This rift between sound and skin confused my senses, and I felt the ground growing unstable underfoot as if it were tilting.

When my unsteady feet regained their confidence, we left Uranus and moved further inside the residential part of town. Walking meant interrupting the city's soporific reminisces, our footsteps the only sound echoing quietly down that road sunken in its summer siesta. Passing by cars from assorted ages, we finally arrived at the Neptune post, which marked the entrance to the forest.

Inside the forest that spread outward from Neptune, the sight of the women advancing slowly around me began to merge curiously with images of saints. This transformation also extended to the forest leading to Pluto. The sun shining directly through the gaps in the leaves formed narrow strips, which resembled the light filtering through church windows. The trees formed cloisters, and the air slipping past silently was cool and soft. The path that led to the post for the planet named for Hades was as hushed as if it were transporting us to the gates of the underworld itself. We spotted some fellow walkers, but they too were sunken in meditation or prayer like those making their way through a church.

The forest was both quieter and more full of life than the city. The trees rustled, and bird calls echoed from near and far. Let off his leash, the truffle dog stretched, immediately acclimatizing to the forest air. He ran circles around us, sprightly as a dancer, before bounding off into the forest with a frontrunner's freedom. As we walked, the distance between us billowed and lapsed, and the movement of our feet overlapped with the sound of accordion music. Since entering the forest, Agatha's face wore the trace of a smile. Her voice, however, still sounded like it belonged to someone who was lost. When asked if she was okay she would nod, but a shadow cut into her smile. Seeing this, the truffle dog dove between us and pressed his black glossy head against her.

The further we walked, the more our bodies grew accustomed to the rhythmic pattern of light and shadow woven by the trees. I found myself walking close beside Lucia and Katharina. Once again, Lucia wore her unusual necklace: the *nazar boncuğu*, the eye of blue glass. That expressionless eye blinked as it reflected the light filtering through the canopy of trees. Each blink revealed a painful-looking crack running down its center. As I was peering at the necklace, a smile floated quietly to Lucia's face. "This was in one of the photos that Agatha took. I got Ursula to bring it to her collection room, and so it found its way back to me." Her last words — "found its way back to me" — rang in my ears. Today too, Lucia's eyes were the color of the March sky in that far-off place — the hue that wavered on the border between winter and spring. Its paleness, though, evoked a paintbrush laden with gray, leaning toward the silent repudiation that was winter's. But Lucia didn't say anything else about that eye-shaped memory attribute. The memory lay there in her sight, but she'd chosen to remain silent about it. She ran her fingers across the scar in the navy-blue eye, and this, I presumed, was her way of communicating this memory that was illegible to me.

Her back and legs drawn straight as swords, Katharina was walking a few steps ahead. The wheel-shaped earrings dangling from her ears swayed rhythmically with her steps, glinting when the rays of sunlight touched them. "Katharina." When I said her name, she turned to look at me, her face as placid as a mask. Without altering expression, she fell in step with Lucia and me. Her sensitive kindness was of a type that didn't translate easily into words and facial expressions, and she favored language that was as straightforward as her way of walking. Knowing this, I deliberately phrased my question to avoid ambiguities.

"Did you take something from Ursula's room?"

Katharina nodded. "Ursula's storing the wheel of a children's bicycle and a wooden sword from the Christmas market for me in her room. I suspect I won't ever take them."

"Are you just going to leave them there?" Lucia asked.

"I don't know." In contrast with what she was saying, Katharina's voice had a clear, cloudless quality. "They belonged to my dead brother. He used to pretend he was a knight, riding around on that bicycle like it was a horse with the sword at his waist." As she went on, the hard edges of her words softened. "My brother died when he was young, so that's all I remember about him. Even that image of him is something I only have because my parents passed it on." Those memory fragments had already assumed the form of an enduring portrait inside her. Rather than accumulating another attribute, she'd chosen to hang onto that solitary picture of him.

As we passed through the forest, it continued to shroud itself in different layers of ecclesiastic imagery and throw them off again. Eventually the forest path reached Kaiser Wilhelm Park, and we decided to take a short break. The park was an extension of the forest but it contained various pieces of outdoor equipment. We saw stone benches and a semicircular stage, its mouth ajar as if it were napping amid the park's green and water-like stillness. In that park, named for the former German Emperor, there was nobody else in sight. We had the whole place to ourselves.

"I brought some cakes." A gold cake tin like a great goblet was offered to me. The words were Barbara's. Reflexively I took one of the cakes, which were white, thin, and round, so light they seemed they would break apart instantly against my teeth. Biting into it, I found the cake was neither sweet nor salty. It sucked up the moisture in my mouth and dissolved on my tongue. Egged on by Barbara's smile, which seemed redolent with the same sweet fragrance she exuded, I swallowed down the mysterious white substance. "It's like a rice cracker," Nomiya murmured. Out of sight of Barbara, who'd gone back to stand beside Agnes, I nodded in agreement. Standing nearby, Lucia tilted her water bottle so that it reflected the sun, sending rays of light flying here and there in a waterwheel pattern. Katharina passed around a container of pretzels, all shaped like wheels. Mr. Terada took out a jar of konpeito candy, and when Agnes peered at them in curiosity, he gave her a careful explanation of the process by which the confectionery with its three-dimensional star shape was formed.

There was no sign of Ursula. Confused, we looked around the area, plying the landscape around us with our gazes, only to find that one of the trees had come to assume Ursula's likeness.

While standing there with her characteristic treelike stillness, had she become entwined with the forest? Now she took out a Jupitertorte from her bag—how had she carried it here?—and begun to cut it apart. As she was placing the slices on paper napkins, Agnes looked down at the pattern of the cake and said to Ursula in a cutesy voice like a little lamb, "Can I have the one with the rose on it?" The piece of cake bearing the Great Red Spot was handed to her, and then the other slices of Jupitertorte went slipping through space toward outstretched hands. "Agatha!" someone called out to the figure sitting slightly apart from the rest of the group. "Agatha!" "Agatha!" The voices interlocked, frilled with laughter. "Come over here and have some cake." "You're too far away." "You're not Pluto, you know!" The voices overlapped and dissolved like waves, melting into a whirl of color, so it was impossible to distinguish each person's voice. Through those laughing voices, Agatha moved with the truffle dog inside the ring of sedentary people. The air around us was peculiarly bright, and it bounced off the trees, which began to spread soft shadows. The dried ivy entangled in their branches had begun to glisten a luscious green. Even the flowers that had grown weary in the strong sunlight now exuded a gentle scent, their petals assuming the translucence of glass. The murmurs of the birds were not the usual warning announcements, but the high trills of female opera singers. With their calls as accompaniment, the box containing the cake moved through the air from hand to hand, fluttering busily through my vision with the lightness of a butterfly. Laughter like beads of glass spilled from the mouths of the women with their saints' names, and drawn along by them, Nomiya and Mr. Terada also became instruments of laughter, creating harmonies. The truffle dog wagged his tail like a conductor's baton, beating time for the eddying voices. The bright light streaming through the gaps in the leaves flowed down with all the transparent ooze of honey, as if encapsulating the time and place of this afternoon in amber. I, too, was swallowed up by this honey jar moment, succumbing slowly to its sweet gold.

As I was rocked by the illusions floating through this soft air, I sensed someone had sat down quietly next to me. It was Agnes. The girl who usually kept her distance sat on the stone bench alongside me, restlessly moving her body, alternating between hugging her knees to her chest and stretching her legs. It was as if she were performing vocal exercises for speaking. That awkwardness she carried in her gestures was also part of her language. Looking carefully, I saw that she held a wooden sheep in her hand. The sheep was missing a piece from its nose. Its form was etched into my memory: a lamb looking off to the side, wanting to say something.

"Did you bring that with you?" Agnes nodded, stroking the chipped nose with her finger. How many times had she repeated that gesture? The smooth, neat movement of her finger described a psychological arc, too. "It was a present from my dad," she said in a voice so quiet it almost seemed to get lost amid the rustle of the leaves. The little lost lamb given to her by her dead father. "When I was a kid I would often have tantrums. I didn't know to control my emotions or my thoughts. So my dad gave me a sheep, and told me that I was its shepherd. His thinking was: if I were put in charge of going out to look for the solitary sheep that stayed out roaming in the fields, then I might be able to see past my own feelings. I don't know if he meant it as a joke or not, but that was what he said." Then Agnes murmured another secret. "My Mom's postcard shows a picture of the Bismarck Tower—that was something he sent her. The tower where Pluto used to be. I don't think my Mom cares about Pluto at all—she just wanted to see the tower."

Agnes stood up, and ran over light-footedly toward the

stage in the distance. The truffle dog followed immediately after her. Watching the black line of his movement, my eyes were drawn to the figure of someone standing at the vanishing point of my line of perspective. Far off in the distance, beneath the lid of the rock opened like a bivalve, Nomiya was waving. The image came together with the sight of him at Göttingen station the first day he'd arrived, standing there like an icon against a background of green, and then dissolved.

Pluto was there. It stood right next to the Bismarck Tower, which was half hidden by the forest. The shadows of the trees fell on its bronze surface, etched with wavy lines. There was no trace of any of other walkers around, and standing as silent witnesses in front of the bronze post, we actually found ourselves unsure of what to do next. We weren't going to take photographs—we had no desire to gather proof of the existence of this thing that now stood plainly in the place where it had once been. The post in which the model planet was set extended that period of time when Pluto had been considered a planet. As if attesting to its wish to remain within that imaginarium, it blended in perfectly with the scenery around. Touching the bronze of the post, a pattern of cold spread across my skin, eventually melting into warmth. The model of the former Pluto seemed far too robust in this form to be termed a ghost, its roots firmly cast down into that spot beside the tower in the forest.

The tower, which was open only on weekends, combined a white cylindrical and hexagonal column, bringing together our varying images of towers within its singular form. Constructed of stones of white, gray, and a soft, muted peach color, its walls resembled the skin of a white birch, like some failed attempt to become a tree. In Barbara's postcard, the tower stood bathed in fall colors and soft light. Now it was summer. Enveloped as it was in green, the tower seemed far removed from that postcard image. And yet as I watched, the words spilling from the postcard tinted the leaves in front of us red, its memories lending the scene before us an autumnal tinge. In deference to the sign pinned on the door to the tower, we took our masks out. Strangely enough, the patterns on all the women's masks evoked the attributes of the saints bearing their name. Only myself, Nomiya, and Mr. Terada wore plain white masks. "I'll wait with Agatha here. We'll watch the dog. Go and see at the tower without us." After saying this, Ursula sat down beside the Pluto bronze post. From her bag she took out a container wrapped in fabric. I was sure that Agatha's memory attribute was stored inside. Seeing it, Agatha's face took on a quiet demeanor. It wasn't a masklike expression, veiled stiffly in hushed tones, and rather a face that might tremble with waves of emotions but would not break. Agatha would now try to strip from her memory the painful perspective that had distorted the original form of things. Maybe this time, she would finally be able to return to the starting point of her memories. If Agatha's words could only be received by Ursula's silence, maybe this would herald an end to her enduring memory loss.

The attendant at the counter where we bought our entrance tickets informed us in a sleepy tone that there were no other visitors. Letting out a birdlike cry from inside her mask, Agnes pointed at something on one of the walls. It was a sheep carved in wood, a crafty expression on its face. Barbara's eyes softened and she whispered two or three words into her daughter's shell-like ear. The girl put her hand into her pocket, confirming that she still had her attribute with her. Barbara and Agnes walked over to the window and started talking quietly. Without a word, we set foot on the spiral staircase and began our ascent. We'd left the clamor of the forest and the birdsong outside those thick stone walls, and inside a different kind of time was flowing. Inside this tower, named in honor of the country's former chancellor who had attended university in Göttingen, time felt as distant as a fossil.

The interior of the tower was surprisingly devoid of any decoration. I supposed that I'd been picturing the kind of stories one saw woven into tapestries: the spinning imp; the woman brushing the hair that had been growing since she'd first been imprisoned in the tower; the woman dreaming of the world outside, which she could only see through the mirror. These images didn't align with the Bismarck Tower. Nomiya and I plied our gazes like fingers, tracing them carefully over the floors, ceilings, and the joints of the walls. Noticing how our actions mirrored one another's, a smile passed across our lips, almost perceptible from behind the masks. Nomiya's body still repeated this way of looking at things we'd learned in our art history studies, as it had nine years before.

Even with five of us walking around the small hexagonal space, the air remained stolidly bathed in quiet. Far from making our footsteps ring out, the stone floor here absorbed them. There were several black plaques inscribed with quotes from Otto von Bismarck on the walls, silent words that didn't disturb our ears. Words from a time not far from that of Mr. Terada. Facing these words was the bust of Bismarck himself. Was this statue, set in this silence, continually repeating its own words, here in this container of words and memories, in this place of motionless time? Leaving Lucia, who was staring placidly out the window, and Katharina, carefully studying the faded gold letters, we ascended to the floor above.

The spiral staircase distorted any sensations. With each loop we made, our impression of time and place seemed to grow paler and farther away. At the top of the stairs was the roof, with its hexagonal terrace. Looking out at the open landscape before them, Nomiya and Mr. Terada soon fixed their gaze in the direction of the city, and began listing off the names of places. Their words and gazes were directed respectively at Göttingen and 月沈原. Beyond the forest, distant and small, lay a city with two alternative expressions. The scene before us compressed the century-long distance. Yet if the two cities overlapped, like pictures on two layers of glass, they still remained apart from one another. "It's okay if we're outside, right?" Nomiya said, and we all took off our masks, breathing in the air of one of those times—or possibly both, simultaneously. "It's quiet here, without the sound of the cicadas," Mr. Terada said. "The birdsong carries a melody, but it's very light. It dissolves right away in the air. The sound of the cicadas creates acute angles in the summer air, like the lines of a chisel that makes the contours of everything that would otherwise be ready to dissolve in the summer heat stand out in contrast even more. Maybe it's because this place lacks noise to delineate its edges that reality and fantasy can mix together like this during the summer." Turning his soft, deep eyes on me, he smiled. "This tour of the planets has been like the eleventh night's dream." With his arms folded behind his back, Mr. Terada threw his gaze into the distance. I didn't know how far that distance extended.

The next thing I knew, Mr. Terada had disappeared. Any trace of him had vanished quietly into that summer air, where the sun alternated between hard and soft. When I asked Nomiya what had happened, he replied quietly that he suspected Mr. Terada had gone home. Back to his time. Back to some far-off place. Back inside his memories of the city. My words lost their shape, got swallowed up inside my throat. Rather than Mr. Terada's return, my thoughts were focused on how it seemed as though Nomiya's time in Göttingen was also approaching its end. As that bright, powerful fact bumped noisily inside my head, it transformed into a pale sadness that spread throughout my body.

Hearing Lucia and Katharina's voices drawing nearer, as they rose up from further down the stairs, we moved up another flight of stairs, coming out onto the roof of the circular tower. The sound of the women's voices vanished, although there was nothing to interrupt them, and the sunshine was redolent with a glassy quietude. We stood there in that total silence, a place that had been designed for words. At that moment, I felt a sense of guilt—that I'd been carrying around like charcoal smoldering beneath the ash—fall away into nothing. During our planetary pilgrimage, I'd located the existence of that nine-year period within him.

"Do you know everything already?" The moment the words slid from my mouth, Nomiya nodded in agreement.

"I heard from Sawata. I was relieved to hear that my parents and my younger sister made it home. Although the situation with my brother bothers me. He almost drowned once when he was a kid, and afterward he was never fond of the sea. So I'd like to get him out of the water and bring him back to land."

With a calm expression, Nomiya pulled something white and shining out from a pocket in his bag. For a moment, I thought it was a tooth. Subconsciously, I reached into my own pocket and held my own teeth in my hand.

"Is that a scallop shell?"

So white was the shell, its lines so clearly engraved, that it was as if it'd never been in the sea. Nomiya nodded.

"Remember that loop of the city we took after dinner at Ursula's? This is one of the shells the truffle dog dug up during that walk. I picked it as a kind of talisman. Two of them, actually. One for my brother as well?" Those shells that connected with the place where Nomiya was from were memory attributes full of an intense, silent pain. With his body still not yet found, the shell gave a form to the time, which took on a shape that couldn't be represented by symbols alone. "Maybe this will lead me there," Nomiya murmured.

"You'll get there." My words coiled around on themselves to form prayers. "That shell leads back to the place that's yours, not St. James's. You'll find your way home." Nomiya nodded quietly.

If only he, and his family, and the people living nearby, had left the seaside and gone somewhere far above sea level, I found myself thinking. I knew there was no point imagining such a thing, but the feelings that the prayer left unguarded inevitably directed themselves there.

Looking out across the distance, I saw the view with another one imposed on top—a seascape. One September several Marches ago, half a year before I came to Germany, I had visited Ishinomaki. I'd stayed overnight with Akiko, who had returned to Matsushima for a short break from Germany. Her parents had been in her grandparents' house in Matsushima, not returning to Kesennuma. Conversation fell persistently between us like a light rain, but Akiko never touched upon the claw marks left behind by the tsunami, or the sea. After parting with her at the station, I'd boarded a Senseki Line train in the direction of Ishinomaki. There was still a while left before sunset, and as I glimpsed flashes of the scenery through the window, it occurred to me that my destination was blue itself. I wanted to see if I could notice the overlapping layers of blue that Altdorfer had painted. What I had in mind back then wasn't Nomiya himself, but the way he'd described the sea. Arriving at the seaside town, I walked around lost, until finally I saw the sea across a temporal lapse of more than a decade.

Yet the sea that I observed on that day had a quietness totally different from all the videos I'd seen. It kept on moving unaltered, toward the city and the land that still bore its scars.

Its expression confused me. Reflecting that same expression myself, I felt no terror or sadness rising up in me. All I took from the sea in front of me was a great sense of distance. Sunset was drawing closer, but the sky was heavily clouded over, and its gray began to show signs of rain. I returned to Sendai without getting to see the blue I'd been hoping to.

I didn't know where Nomiya's house had been, and I didn't try to visit it that time, either. Even if I had known, I probably wouldn't have been able to get there, since I was thinking not of Nomiya but his words about the blue. The place I visited that day was far from the raging sea—a place not exposed to the sea's black and gray violence, a place far from that which had dragged Nomiya and the others off. Drawing relief from this, I busied myself in getting my ruptured way of life back on track. With time, my days began to look as they had before. Yet the existence of those places that couldn't return to their previous state only grew more pronounced, and the scars that were engraved in both people's bodies and the land itself carried severed memories with them.

What I had been afraid of was the distortions of memory caused by emotions and the passage of time. That was where forgetting began. Time was elapsing, but Nomiya still hadn't been found. What my feet had felt as they'd gone tramping around that seaside town, the scenes my eyes had taken in, the smell of the sea that'd rushed into my nose—these memories didn't remain with me as raw sensations, but morphed into a distant narrative. That oblivion concealed more than just the dead who hadn't returned to land. There were those who'd lost everything in the tsunami, those who'd had to leave everything behind when evacuating from the nuclear contamination zone. This situation, this inability to return, was being forgotten little by little in those places removed from the coast, away from the nuclear power plant. The rift between such people, and all those who continued in their quiet yet dedicated search for those who'd been lost to the sea and those things connected to them, was simply too great.

All along, it hadn't been about the pain of the memories, but the guilt I felt for my distance from them. Tracing the contours of the teeth with my fingers, feeling their edges and forms, I turned to face the time that had been Nomiya's. For the first time ever, I felt it—the sadness, the unfairness of his death, and his inability to return home. The nine years pressed upon me clamorously. With my eyes trained on the view, so I wouldn't be distracted by these sensations, I told him briefly about visiting his hometown. The sea I'd seen from the distance—the blue lying behind an expanse of gray, dusted with sparkling particles of light. "I saw the sea, but I didn't get to see its blue. Not like in *The Battle of Alexander at Issus*."

"That's a shame." The sound of his laughter gently cracked the silent summer air.

"It's two forty-six in the afternoon," Nomiya murmured, his voice quiet and clear. Two forty-six p.m.: the time of day to which the vanishing point was set. I thought of the times and places that had been ripped away. Looking down at the city from the top of the tower, I superimposed the scene from Altdorfer's painting onto it. My gaze became a bird, directed at the two planes of blue, above and below. Not taking flight but observing from this fixed perspective, I watched the movements of the avalanching colors and the deepening blue, and at the same time, I saw the scene of a faraway sea connected with it across the distance. Nomiya's quiet presence grew fainter, as if dissolving into the blue of the sea and the sky. I couldn't turn my head to make sure. His presence became entangled in the patchwork folds of memory, where so many different times were connected with one another, and then he grew further away. My prayer that he'd return home became the invisible thread that tethered my memories. Perhaps Nomiya wasn't here anymore. The teeth began clinking in my hand. The sound resembled a lament, vibrating up through my skin and reverberating in my eardrums. The wind that whistled past my ears carried on it a distant rustling of paper. The scene superimposed translucently upon this one was that world of blue that I never got to see, calling out from afar. Now, from over a great distance, that blue came slipping this way. From my fixed avian vantage point, I held those blues on top of one another in my vision, waiting for them to disappear.

New Directions Paperbooks — a partial listing

Adonis, Songs of Mihyar the Damascene
César Aira, Ghosts
 An Episode in the Life of a Landscape Painter
Ryunosuke Akutagawa, Kappa
Will Alexander, Refractive Africa
Osama Alomar, The Teeth of the Comb
Guillaume Apollinaire, Selected Writings
Jessica Au, Cold Enough for Snow
Paul Auster, The Red Notebook
Ingeborg Bachmann, Malina
Honoré de Balzac, Colonel Chabert
Djuna Barnes, Nightwood
Charles Baudelaire, The Flowers of Evil*
Bei Dao, City Gate, Open Up
Yevgenia Belorusets, Lucky Breaks
Rafael Bernal, His Name Was Death
Mei-Mei Berssenbrugge, Empathy
Max Blecher, Adventures in Immediate Irreality
Jorge Luis Borges, Labyrinths
 Seven Nights
Coral Bracho, Firefly Under the Tongue*
Kamau Brathwaite, Ancestors
Anne Carson, Glass, Irony & God
 Wrong Norma
Horacio Castellanos Moya, Senselessness
Camilo José Cela, Mazurka for Two Dead Men
Louis-Ferdinand Céline
 Death on the Installment Plan
 Journey to the End of the Night
Inger Christensen, alphabet
Julio Cortázar, Cronopios and Famas
Jonathan Creasy (ed.), Black Mountain Poems
Robert Creeley, If I Were Writing This
H.D., Selected Poems
Guy Davenport, 7 Greeks
Amparo Dávila, The Houseguest
Osamu Dazai, The Flowers of Buffoonery
 No Longer Human
 The Setting Sun
Anne de Marcken
 It Lasts Forever and Then It's Over
Helen DeWitt, The Last Samurai
 Some Trick
José Donoso, The Obscene Bird of Night
Robert Duncan, Selected Poems
Eça de Queirós, The Maias
Juan Emar, Yesterday

William Empson, 7 Types of Ambiguity
Mathias Énard, Compass
Shusaku Endo, Deep River
Jenny Erpenbeck, Go, Went, Gone
 Kairos
Lawrence Ferlinghetti
 A Coney Island of the Mind
Thalia Field, Personhood
F. Scott Fitzgerald, The Crack-Up
Rivka Galchen, Little Labors
Forrest Gander, Be With
Romain Gary, The Kites
Natalia Ginzburg, The Dry Heart
Henry Green, Concluding
Marlen Haushofer, The Wall
Victor Heringer, The Love of Singular Men
Felisberto Hernández, Piano Stories
Hermann Hesse, Siddhartha
Takashi Hiraide, The Guest Cat
Yoel Hoffmann, Moods
Susan Howe, My Emily Dickinson
 Concordance
Bohumil Hrabal, I Served the King of England
Qurratulain Hyder, River of Fire
Sonallah Ibrahim, That Smell
Rachel Ingalls, Mrs. Caliban
Christopher Isherwood, The Berlin Stories
Fleur Jaeggy, Sweet Days of Discipline
Alfred Jarry, Ubu Roi
B.S. Johnson, House Mother Normal
James Joyce, Stephen Hero
Franz Kafka, Amerika: The Man Who Disappeared
Yasunari Kawabata, Dandelions
Mieko Kanai, Mild Vertigo
John Keene, Counternarratives
Kim Hyesoon, Autobiography of Death
Heinrich von Kleist, Michael Kohlhaas
Taeko Kono, Toddler-Hunting
László Krasznahorkai, Satantango
 Seiobo There Below
Ágota Kristóf, The Illiterate
Eka Kurniawan, Beauty Is a Wound
Mme. de Lafayette, The Princess of Clèves
Lautréamont, Maldoror
Siegfried Lenz, The German Lesson
Alexander Lernet-Holenia, Count Luna

Denise Levertov, Selected Poems
Li Po, Selected Poems
Clarice Lispector, An Apprenticeship
   The Hour of the Star
   The Passion According to G. H.
Federico García Lorca, Selected Poems*
Nathaniel Mackey, Splay Anthem
Xavier de Maistre, Voyage Around My Room
Stéphane Mallarmé, Selected Poetry and Prose*
Javier Marías, Your Face Tomorrow (3 volumes)
Bernadette Mayer, Midwinter Day
Carson McCullers, The Member of the Wedding
Fernando Melchor, Hurricane Season
   Paradais
Thomas Merton, New Seeds of Contemplation
   The Way of Chuang Tzu
Henri Michaux, A Barbarian in Asia
Henry Miller, The Colossus of Maroussi
   Big Sur & the Oranges of Hieronymus Bosch
Yukio Mishima, Confessions of a Mask
   Death in Midsummer
Eugenio Montale, Selected Poems*
Vladimir Nabokov, Laughter in the Dark
Pablo Neruda, The Captain's Verses*
   Love Poems*
Charles Olson, Selected Writings
George Oppen, New Collected Poems
Wilfred Owen, Collected Poems
Hiroko Oyamada, The Hole
José Emilio Pacheco, Battles in the Desert
Michael Palmer, Little Elegies for Sister Satan
Nicanor Parra, Antipoems*
Boris Pasternak, Safe Conduct
Octavio Paz, Poems of Octavio Paz
Victor Pelevin, Omon Ra
Fernando Pessoa
   The Complete Works of Alberto Caeiro
Alejandra Pizarnik
   Extracting the Stone of Madness
Robert Plunket, My Search for Warren Harding
Ezra Pound, The Cantos
   New Selected Poems and Translations
Qian Zhongshu, Fortress Besieged
Raymond Queneau, Exercises in Style
Olga Ravn, The Employees
Herbert Read, The Green Child
Kenneth Rexroth, Selected Poems
Keith Ridgway, A Shock

Rainer Maria Rilke
   Poems from the Book of Hours
Arthur Rimbaud, Illuminations*
   A Season in Hell and The Drunken Boat*
Evelio Rosero, The Armies
Fran Ross, Oreo
Joseph Roth, The Emperor's Tomb
Raymond Roussel, Locus Solus
Ihara Saikaku, The Life of an Amorous Woman
Nathalie Sarraute, Tropisms
Jean-Paul Sartre, Nausea
Kathryn Scanlan, Kick the Latch
Delmore Schwartz
   In Dreams Begin Responsibilities
W. G. Sebald, The Emigrants
   The Rings of Saturn
Anne Serre, The Governesses
Patti Smith, Woolgathering
Stevie Smith, Best Poems
   Novel on Yellow Paper
Gary Snyder, Turtle Island
Muriel Spark, The Driver's Seat
   The Public Image
Maria Stepanova, In Memory of Memory
Wislawa Szymborska, How to Start Writing
Antonio Tabucchi, Pereira Maintains
Junichiro Tanizaki, The Maids
Yoko Tawada, The Emissary
   Scattered All over the Earth
Dylan Thomas, A Child's Christmas in Wales
   Collected Poems
Thuan, Chinatown
Rosemary Tonks, The Bloater
Tomas Tranströmer, The Great Enigma
Leonid Tsypkin, Summer in Baden-Baden
Tu Fu, Selected Poems
Elio Vittorini, Conversations in Sicily
Rosmarie Waldrop, The Nick of Time
Robert Walser, The Tanners
Eliot Weinberger, An Elemental Thing
   Nineteen Ways of Looking at Wang Wei
Nathanael West, The Day of the Locust
   Miss Lonelyhearts
Tennessee Williams, The Glass Menagerie
   A Streetcar Named Desire
William Carlos Williams, Selected Poems
Alexis Wright, Praiseworthy
Louis Zukofsky, "A"

*BILINGUAL EDITION

For a complete listing, request a free catalog from New Directions, 80 8th Avenue, New York, NY 10011
or visit us online at ndbooks.com